Leadership, Ethics and Paradigm Shifts

— A Motivational Guide to Leadership,

in the 21st Century

Published by:

Colin Maxwell

ISBN

Colin Maxwell

During the preparation of this book, several books were reviewed, but unfortunately, due to an incident, they were lost. I extend my gratitude to the publishers and authors of those books, and the sources I accessed on the Internet. I apologize for not being able to mention their names in the bibliography.

Dedication

This is my fourth book on business management. Like its predecessors, it is dedicated to my family and friends, who have always encouraged me to write books on leadership and management in the 21st century. Hopefully, this book will benefit students, laypeople, businesspersons, and professionals alike.

About the Author

Colin Maxwell, an established business consultant and author, holds an honors degree in Economics from the University of Leeds, England, and a PhD in Business Administration from Pacific Southern University, California, USA. He is a member of the Institute of Chartered Accountants (England and Wales) and a Life Member of the Institute of Professional Managers and Administrators (UK). Colin Maxwell is recognized in several esteemed international publications as a professional of repute.

Fluent in multiple languages, Colin Maxwell's international experience spans Business Consulting, Corporate Analysis, Management Information Systems, Training and Development, Valuation and Sale of Business, Raising Venture Capital, and Administration. He advocates that robust theory underpins effective practice, and emphasizes the continuous scope for improvement.

In his role, Colin Maxwell conducts lectures and seminars, and participates in radio interviews on various topics, including Business, HR Management, Business Ethics, Business Law, Economics, and Accounting. His audience comprises graduates, seasoned businessmen, and professionals.

This book follows his highly acclaimed and authoritative leadership and business management manuals. "Leadership, Ethics, and Paradigm Shifts" represents another effort to guide global leaders. It emphasizes that beyond mere numbers, understanding people's recruitment, training, and motivation within an ethical team environment, is critical for corporate success or failure. It argues against disrespect or demotivation of employees by supervisors and others, underscoring that an ethical approach to business is imperative.

Colin Maxwell is dedicated to working with business persons, leaders, managers, and other professionals, employing a pragmatic approach to resolving their challenges.

Preface

This, my fourth book on leadership and business management, is intended to provide easy, directed reading for those interested in grasping the essentials of Leadership, General Management, Stress and Anger Management, Customer Service, Family Business and Succession Planning, Homebased Business Organizations, Retirement Planning, and other areas of business. The earlier editions of this book were reviewed by businessmen, professionals, students, and others. This edition is based on their feedback and reviews. In the 21st century, life in business and elsewhere, is expected to become increasingly volatile and complex.

Acknowledgments

I am indebted to Maurice Pinto; Mark Pinto, M.B.A., Ch.FC.; Krishna Prasad, BSc.; Aley Thomas, M.B.A.; Eusebia Menezes-Pinto, M.A., M.Sc.; Maurice Coutinho, V.P., American Express; Josie Gelacio, B.Ed.; Mari-Jane Sutton; Aaron Pinto, M.Sc.; Esther Pinto, Ms.ISM.; and others whose names I may have overlooked but to whom I am eternally grateful.

Table of Contents

CHAPTER 1 – 21st Century Leadership and the Impact of the Internet

The emergence of the Internet has greatly impacted the way we communicate with one another in the business world and elsewhere. To operate successfully, one must have suitable computer hardware and software and the right people in place, i.e., those who have been selected on merit (including the ability to operate effectively within a team environment) rather than relationships, friendship, or other irrelevant criteria. The Internet may be the "holy grail" of business, enabling people and organizations to be extremely effective.

The Business Environment Involves Human Beings

Information is fundamental to success, but it must be relevant, accurate, timely, clearly understood, and imparted appropriately, to the right people, or else its usefulness will be diminished. The effective use of relevant, accurate, and timely information promotes business and personal success; honest feedback can be very helpful.

Excessive use of the Internet may undermine the value of human contact, i.e., people may communicate via the Internet in circumstances where face-to-face contact is advisable – such as, when they are seated close to one another! Sometimes, members of the same department of a firm spend a considerable amount of time communicating via email, when it would be more productive to have face-to-face meetings, at least on some occasions.

In business, we sometimes forget that we operate within a human environment, where emotions play a part because people, unlike robots, have feelings. Therefore, one must understand the nature of the people one has to deal with, what makes them tick, and what upsets them. If you approach somebody who is time-conscious, make sure you are punctual and precise; otherwise, you will irritate him or her and fail to achieve the desired result. Whereas some people emphasize money, others are more conscious of their status, how much they are liked in a firm, how much freedom and power they have, or whether the firm operates in an ethical manner or not. One should bear this in mind, when dealing with people. Most people tend to exaggerate or lie in order to impress others regarding their actual or potential achievements. This being the case, it is important to read people well in order to gain a strong foothold in business.

Priorities and Establishing Beneficial Relationships

Setting and pursuing goals necessitates commitment. Individuals need to recognize their priorities and act accordingly. Whether one aims for increased power, skills, contacts, money, or other aspirations, being prepared to relinquish certain things is essential for setting and achieving more meaningful objectives. Often, people are reluctant to skip a crucial business meeting to spend quality time with their families. Instead, they rationalize that attending the meeting accelerates their career advancement, ultimately benefiting their families.

Embrace creativity: Utilize your imagination to connect people in such a way, that all parties involved reap benefits. Those who gain from these connections will eventually understand the advantages they've received and should be in a position to offer some form of reciprocation. Concentrate on the well-being of the connected parties instead of focusing solely on your own benefits.

The business environment is volatile, encompassing a variety of distinct requirements. Companies may need to undergo restructuring or downsizing to cope with competitive pressures. Employees often switch jobs due to the rarity of job satisfaction and the near absence of job security. To mitigate such disruptions, managers should motivate their employees by fostering respect, teamwork, care, sharing, offering training, fair compensation packages, increasing responsibilities, and challenging assignments. This approach encourages employees to solve problems and feel valued for their contributions. Treating employees like family and showing genuine care can yield significant rewards in loyalty and performance.

It's important to acknowledge those who contribute to your success. Being conscious of your weaknesses and striving to eliminate them is crucial. In a world of intense competition – both among employees and against external competitors, like other suppliers of similar products or services – one must be both intelligent and swift in approach to avoid falling behind. The adage "Slow and steady wins the race" is a formula for mediocrity, which is not applicable in such a dynamic environment; speed is essential, but not at the cost of quality. The intelligence and quickness of an individual might inspire envy rather than respect, but this should not adversely affect the firm. Communications should be concise, and the time between recognizing a problem and solving it should be minimized.

Be aware of those who genuinely support you and are ready to stand by you in times of difficulty. Similarly, recognize your adversaries, and attempt to convert them into allies through kindness. Spend time understanding people's strengths and weaknesses to know whom to depend on in various situations. Remembering this can help your career progression.

Build relationships with colleagues whose job functions are relevant to yours because they can help lighten your workload. For example, there might be instances when you need urgent assistance from someone in the mailroom. In such cases, contacting them directly is often more efficient than going through your manager.

Never compromise on quality or ethics. If the budget is insufficient for certain tasks, communicate with the relevant authority to revise it accordingly. Reducing costs *at the expense of the firm's reputation is completely unacceptable!*

Pay attention to the timing of calls you receive, as this can help avoid the inconvenience of a telephone tag. People have different preferences for calling times; some prefer mornings, while others might call later in the day. Noting these preferences can make your phone time more efficient.

Customers – An Enigma!

Developing a relationship with clients hinges on trust, results, and adapting to their evolving needs. Upholding ethics is crucial; therefore, building and maintaining a profitable client base through unethical practices is unequivocally unacceptable.

Customer service should be exemplary in a world where minimal errors are expected. At times, it's wise to apologize to the customer, along with a compensatory benefit, demonstrating your commitment to their satisfaction under any circumstances. Companies should strive for a zero-tolerance policy regarding mistakes, as they can be costly and frustrating to customers, suppliers, and others, potentially damaging the business's reputation and negatively impacting the bottom line. However, it's important to acknowledge that humans are prone to errors – a trait not shared by robots.

Listening attentively to your customers is essential in order to meet their specific (and reasonable) needs, ultimately enhancing the bottom line. Occasionally, a customer might recognize the need for your product but hesitate to use it due to concerns about displacing an existing, profitable product. For instance, a retailer successfully selling the George Foreman Grill might be hesitant to replace it with your new, unproven product. In such cases, persuade the customer to sell both products, observe which one yields higher profits over a set period, and consider offering an additional incentive. Alternatively, you may need to "create" a need for a customer by introducing products like a cellular phone, a digital camera, or a combination of both, especially when the customer has never felt the need for such products and is content with their current possessions.

Ideas, Decisions, and Implementation

Individuals can only claim to have comprehensive knowledge, about their role within an organization. Thus, it's commendable to acknowledge one's limitations and strive to overcome them. Great ideas hold no value unless executed promptly. When proposing an idea, ensure that it is effectively presented to the decision maker, capturing the latter's attention and prompting necessary actions. The most impactful ideas often need their creator's support, making them harder to replicate. Sharing your ideas and assisting others, can foster mutual gratitude and support when most needed.

Decision-making should be based on extensive, relevant, accurate, and timely information. This process involves analyzing the data and drawing on experience and intuition, rather than relying solely on logic. It's important to recognize that people often incorporate intuition in decision-making, especially in uncertain situations. Decisions should always be made after careful deliberation. However, correcting poor decisions is crucial, such as reversing a hiring mistake if the employee fails to meet the required standards.

A degree of nervousness can drive conscientious individuals to work harder, in line with their objectives, whether in business, personal life, or sports. For instance, not feeling somewhat nervous might indicate an underestimation of a task, similar to Foreman's approach against Ali or Nastase's approach against Borg, at Wimbledon in 1976.

Meetings offer excellent opportunities for exposure, especially when well-prepared and allowing others to share their perspectives. Embrace these moments to express yourself and don't shy away from tasks that stretch your current abilities. Showing initiative is commendable, provided you can deliver on the task.

When meeting with outsiders, it's advisable to choose neutral venues to negate their 'home court advantage.' Designating a specific restaurant as a meeting place is a practical approach. Continuously observing people to understand their nature and style is beneficial. Being alert can provide insights that maximize opportunities. Generosity, such as offering to pay the bill at a restaurant, can reflect positively, on your character.

In networking, aim for genuine connections rather than overtly seeking business opportunities. People can sense when they are being used for someone's self-interest, which can damage potential relationships.

Working Style, Fairness, and Loyalty

Successful individuals understand that it is sometimes necessary to step on people's toes. They focus on being effective rather than just being "nice." When applying for a job, these individuals often include references that can vouch for their character traits, such as a kind heart, as evidenced by their volunteer work with the homeless and needy.

People need to be conscious of their working style and the times when they are most productive, whether it be certain times of the day, week, or year. They can enhance their performance by structuring their meetings and assignments around these peak times. Bosses appreciate employees who think critically and augment their abilities and performance, thereby contributing value to the business rather than those who consistently agree with them.

We all encounter crises occasionally. Some learn from these experiences and improve their performance, while others lament their circumstances.

Managers and others should always strive for fairness in their interactions. Treating others as you would want to be treated will bring blessings in both your business and personal life. This may not always translate to monetary gain, but it brings a type of inner satisfaction that is hard to measure financially. It's also crucial to surround yourself with a circle of true friends.

Individuality, Intelligence, and Talent

Every individual is unique; people have different talents. Logic is not the only proof of a person's intelligence. Accordingly, people should be selected for assignments based on the requirements of specific assignments, their flexibility, and their ability to operate as members of the team in question.

Needs and Wants

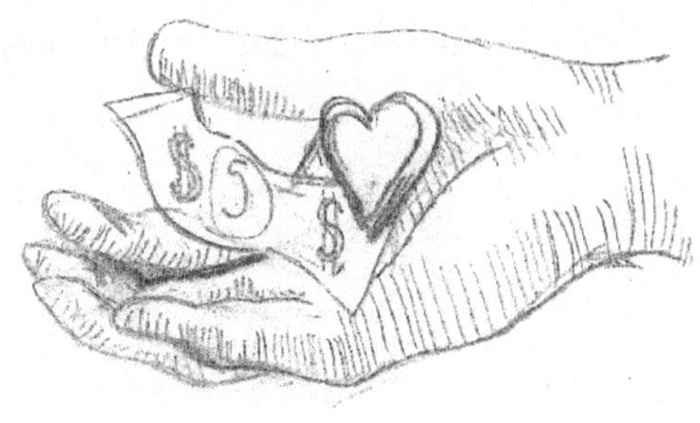

People's needs and wants evolve over time. While money often plays a crucial role in this equation, other vital elements include respect, motivation, a sense of belonging, companionship, and a level of achievement that aligns with personal goals.

The Employment Contract

The employment contract should clearly outline the employee's responsibilities and the corresponding compensation package for their commitment. However, it's important to acknowledge that such contracts can only be partially comprehensive. Inevitably, there are implied terms that stem from the mutual expectations of both parties and ethical considerations. Effective communication, both in words and actions, is crucial in supplementing the contract. This communication fosters goal alignment and enhances the satisfaction of all involved parties.

In any form of relationship, there is an implicit contract, that should be respected. Both sides must recognize their responsibilities and value the opportunities that arise from the relationship in question.

When appraising an employee, honesty is paramount, whether the appraisal is formal or informal. Avoiding direct communication or delegating the task of conveying feedback about an employee's performance to others is professionally inappropriate and should be avoided.

An Individual's Work Area

An individual's work area offers a glimpse into his or her personality. It is essential to extend common courtesy to the occupant of a work area, not only during a visit, but also before and after it. Maintaining a neat and organized workspace is crucial. It's also important to consider Feng Shui, the Chinese art of arrangement. This approach enhances harmony and efficiency, emphasizing the importance of avoiding clutter.

The 'Johari Window' concept explores the contrast between our self-perception and how others perceive us. It reveals that there are aspects of our personality that are unknown to us and others, as well as parts that we choose not to reveal, often due to a desire for privacy.

People form impressions of us based on various factors: our behavior, the state of our work area, our dress and communication style, and our body language. Similarly, impressions of a company are shaped by its interactions with employees, customers, and suppliers and the physical layout and style of its premises, including decoration, space allocation, and other considerations.

It is advisable for individuals to seek employment with companies whose management style and operations align with their own style and personality. Such alignment minimizes friction, all else being equal.

We must engage in roles that match our abilities; otherwise, we risk underperforming due to miscasting. Taking calculated risks is sometimes advisable, as the adage "nothing ventured, nothing gained" suggests. Managers and employees are entrusted with certain powers, which should be exercised in alignment with corporate objectives.

Teams, "Knowledge Workers" and Other Matters

Teams should be organized based on the specific tasks they need to accomplish. It is crucial for team members to have complementary skills, enabling them to produce effective solutions synergistically.

Peter Drucker, a highly esteemed management thinker of his era, coined the term *"knowledge workers."* These individuals are endowed with intelligence and knowledge, which can significantly benefit their organization. In return, they deserve recognition, respect, and fair compensation. These workers rely on the organization for their livelihood, while the organization depends on their contributions to achieve corporate objectives. Drucker posited that our world is increasingly becoming knowledge centric, and that knowledge workers play a pivotal role in transforming management into a distinguished and influential field.

In their seminal work, *"The Knowledge-Creating Company: How Japanese Companies Create the Dynamics of Innovation,"* Nonaka and Takeuchi discuss the gradual process of knowledge creation. This process involves acquiring knowledge from both internal and external sources, and then developing it further. They also highlight the crucial role of middle management as a bridge connecting senior managers and frontline workers.

Charles Handy, a renowned author, accurately foresaw several trends, such as the rise of outsourcing, telecommuting, the intellectual capital movement, knowledge workers, and virtual project teams. In his book "Intellectual Capital: The New Wealth of Organizations," Thomas Stewart explores the concept of intellectual capital and its components. He asserts that it consists of:

a) Human Capital, which is embodied in the knowledge and skills of employees;

b) Customer Capital, representing the value of the company's ongoing relationships with its customers;

c) Structural Capital, which pertains to the knowledge preserved within the company.

Ethics

An organization should never compromise its principles. Outdated procedures need to be carefully reviewed and revised. Profitable growth is usually the goal, though not at the expense of compromised principles; otherwise, the organization will be regarded as lacking in substance, and success may be short-lived, and eventually wiped out, by lawsuits and damages. Pursuing profitable growth should not adversely affect working conditions, or the environment.

Individuals and organizations should understand that unethical practices will not be tolerated under any circumstances whatsoever. While some individuals engage in unethical practices that benefit the organization to which they belong, there are others, who engage in unethical practices, for personal gains, at the expense of corporate welfare.

Several business enterprises offer seasonal employment opportunities to students who are in need of industrial experience to complement their education and make them more marketable on graduation. This provides a win-win situation for the business enterprise and the student in question. In my opinion, the student should be paid a nominal salary as a token of appreciation, assuming that the student displays a keen interest in the job rather than a tendency to merely go through the motions in an attempt to boost his or her resume'. There will indeed be a cost associated with training the student. It is also true that the student will add value to the enterprise. Surely, the enterprise would not offer the student in question an assignment merely on the basis of love for their fellow man, or on religious grounds!

People, Communication, Negotiation and Related Matters

Individuals who have been selected on the basis of merit, including their ability to function effectively in a team environment, rather than through friendships or other irrelevant factors, are an organization's key resource. Consequently, it's essential to provide them with ongoing training and encourage their participation in decision-making processes and brainstorming sessions, thus alleviating management's workload. They should be motivated through respect, care, opportunities for collaboration, challenging tasks, increasing responsibilities based on competence, teamwork, and fair compensation. This approach aligns their actions with the organization's goals. Acknowledging their efforts, performance, and both classical and emotional intelligence – which can be as crucial as practical wisdom – is vital.

Managers should balance their focus between current operations and future planning. This planning should depend on the need for sustainable, profitable growth, leveraging core competencies, and acquiring new talent through employment, subcontracting, or other avenues. Awareness of current and future trends in the business world, based on facts, experience, and intuition, is crucial for effective management.

Communication and feedback are fundamental in any relationship between spouses, friends, employees and managers, employees and customers, suppliers, or even competitors. Ethical considerations are paramount.

Negotiation is a core aspect of both life and business. Parties involved in negotiations should aim to strengthen their relationship through mutually beneficial outcomes, fostering teamwork and cooperation. Demonstrating genuine concern for the welfare of others can promote mutual success.

Life's complexities often allow for simplification by those involved. Ultimately, the key lies in one's approach to problem-solving and recognizing that some issues, like anger management, may never be fully resolved but can be satisfactorily addressed.

Leadership, Vision and Approach

Leaders aim to transform their vision into reality by sharing it with their team. It's crucial for them to be ethical and to lead by example, thereby inspiring their followers to evolve into leaders themselves. Recognizing the importance of merit-based selection, particularly for team compatibility, and nurturing and motivating team members, is key to fostering profitable growth. Training and development are paramount in these times of constant change, characterized by restructuring and downsizing. It's the people, rather than just financial resources, that determine the success or failure of an organization.

Leaders should balance optimism with realism to avoid the pitfalls of fantasy. They need to embrace positive change and earn respect through their actions and performance. Leaders can achieve desired results and foster individual and corporate growth by using, rather than abusing, the power entrusted to them. Leading by example and empowering others is more effective than relying solely on rhetoric. Effective communication, encompassing the right words, tone, and body language, often separates great leaders from poor ones.

Patricia King, in her book "Never Work for a Jerk!", asserts that incompetent bosses can lead to significant losses for both individuals and companies. Often, employees are selected or promoted based on criteria unrelated to merit, resulting in chaos and suboptimal outcomes. These ill-equipped individuals struggle with decision-making, training, and people skills, leading to a scenario akin to "the blind leading the blind."

Talented employees frequently leave organizations, due to a need for more personal respect and care. This issue persists across different jobs, as many supervisors and managers need more proper training. Research shows that many employees are dissatisfied with their treatment by superiors. Managers are critical in whether employees stay and prosper in a firm or leave, taking their knowledge, experience, and contacts to competitors.

Marcus Buckingham and Curt Coffman emphasize, "People leave managers, not companies." A considerable amount of investment is made to retain talent through better pay and perks, but ultimately, turnover is often a management issue: If there's a high turnover rate, look first to your managers. *Are they driving people away?*

Bad bosses can significantly harm the emotional well-being and productivity of their employees. When they criticize, insult, or degrade staff in front of others, exhibit excessive pickiness while assuming their own perfection, or fail to share necessary information, it negatively impacts both the professional and the personal lives of their employees. Such issues should not be allowed to escalate. Some managers are overly controlling, suspicious, pushy, critical, and difficult to please, forgetting that workers are free agents, not fixed assets. This behavior can lead to employees quitting, often due to the accumulation of what might seem like minor issues. While people leave jobs for various opportunities or due to circumstances, many would choose to stay if they were treated well enough to justify continuing their employment.

The cost of losing a talented employee is multifaceted. It includes the expenses of finding and training a replacement, the interim loss of productivity, the potential loss of clients and industry contacts, the diminished morale among coworkers, the risk of trade secrets being shared with competitors, and the potential damage to the company's reputation. Every departing employee can become an ambassador for the company, for better or worse.

Organizations need to have rules and leaders who enforce them. However, these rules should encourage creativity and profitable growth and must operate within the bounds of good working conditions and environmental care. Equally important is respect for all individuals in the organization, not just supervisors and managers. This respect fosters a sense of worth, well-being, and belonging within the company's family of workers.

CHAPTER 2 – Ethical Leadership: An Oxymoron?

Leadership encompasses vision, guidance, motivation, and achieving desirable outcomes. *Ethical* leadership further incorporates aspects of morality, principles, integrity, values, compassion, sharing, a commitment to sustainability ("a green approach"), and the significance of participative decision-making.

Abraham Lincoln, the 16th President of the United States, adeptly guided the nation through the tumultuous American Civil War, ensuring the preservation of the Union and the abolition of slavery. He once articulated his moral compass by stating, *"When I do good, I feel good; when I do bad, I feel bad. That's my religion."* What guiding principles shape your actions?

Albert Schweitzer, distinguished as a theologian, musician, philosopher, and physician, was honored with the Nobel Peace Prize for his *"Reverence for Life"* philosophy. He dedicated much of his life to developing a practical ethical philosophy for the betterment of society, firmly believing in humans' ethical obligation to assist, rather than harm, others.

Wystan Hugh Auden celebrated as one of the 20th century's most eminent writers and poets, delved into themes of morality, love, politics, and citizenship in his works. He once remarked, *"We are here on earth to do good for others. What the others are here for, I don't know,"* highlighting his commitment to altruism.

William Lloyd Garrison, a prominent American journalist, social reformer, and cofounder of the American Antislavery Society, also championed the women's suffrage movement. He asserted that the success of any significant moral endeavor is independent of sheer numbers.

In an ideal world, questions like *"Did you lie, steal, or cheat?"* would have straightforward answers. However, reality is often more complex. For instance, downloading free music from the internet initially deprives artists and distributors of income, but it could eventually boost sales through referrals. This scenario raises the question: does such downloading constitute stealing or cheating? From my perspective, as an author, I welcome people reading significant portions of my books for free online. In line with this, I have made substantial parts of my book available for complimentary downloads on various internet archives.

Another ethical dilemma to consider is the use of sports supplements. To what extent is their consumption ethical? If they are not legally prohibited, does that automatically render them ethically acceptable?

Black, White, and Gray

Right and wrong are often perceived as black and white, absolute, pure, and uncomplicated. However, our ethical system and behavior are influenced by many factors, such as cultural background, upbringing, education, ego, environment, circumstances, and associated stress. This intricate web of influences inevitably leads to the development of gray areas – those realms where explicit rulings or guidance are not readily available. Seen from another perspective, there are various shades of black and white, akin to the experience of selecting different tones of black or white paint at a paint shop, or choosing a black or white suit at a clothing store. It is essential to strive for ethical standards that surpass those of our peers and other organizations.

The image one projects is intricately linked to how one navigates these black, white, and gray areas. Keeping this in mind is crucial while continuously striving for ethical improvement.

Ego and Language

As adults, we often carry an ego and utilize our communication skills to justify our behavior, primarily focusing on achieving our goals. This innate selfishness, combined with influences from friends, family, and our environment, introduces numerous gray areas into our interactions and decision-making processes.

Business Ethics

In business, it is often perceived that the primary focus is on financial gain, rather than, on other factors. This perspective aligns with the shareholder approach, which prioritizes the interests of stockholders, in contrast to the stakeholder approach, which considers the needs of a broader group, including employees, customers, suppliers, the government, and the environment.

When it comes to a potential sale, the question arises: is it incumbent upon the seller to disclose all significant details about the product or service in question? How should the seller respond to inquiries – should he or she provide precise answers to each question, or is it sufficient to address the general intent of the inquiries? Conversely, does the onus fall on the buyer, to thoroughly investigate the advantages and disadvantages of their potential purchase, through diligent research? These considerations represent a complex and ambiguous area in business ethics.

Good Faith

From an ethical standpoint, utmost good faith is paramount. It is essential that the contract accurately mirrors the spirit of the agreement; therefore, it should be revised to align with the originally agreed-upon terms, regardless of the absence of a legal mandate. Emphasizing a win-win scenario for all involved parties is key to ensuring profitable growth.

Right and Wrong – Myth or Reality?

Business decisions frequently involve complex scenarios that are not entirely ethical or unethical. As a result, making the right choice can be challenging, which contradicts the simplicity suggested by many philosophically based case studies. Moral values like respect, honesty, fairness, and responsibility should guide our ethical behavior. However, these values are often overlooked during times of stress and confusion when adhering to one's principles is most crucial. We will delve into this topic in more detail later on.

Dilemmas and Mazes of Fiction/Nonfiction

1. Business ethics revolves around navigating dilemmas that frequently lack a clear distinction between right and wrong.

2. Leaders often find themselves addressing potential conflicts of interest, improper utilization of resources, contract mismanagement, unfulfilled promises, and excessive demands on resources, including personnel.

Business Ethics and Leadership

Business ethics necessitates an awareness of social responsibility, which includes tackling societal issues like poverty, crime, environmental protection, equal rights, public health, and enhancing education. This is reflected in concepts such as stakeholder theory, the focus on public relations, improved human resource management, and others. Our concern centers around people, the planet, and how we generate profits.

Regrettably, many business schools offer training in business ethics, favoring a philosophical approach, over a practical one. This approach requires reconsideration, in the light of real-world experiences. Regular and frequent oaths related to ethical compliance represent a step in the right direction. However, they are not a definitive guarantee of ethical behavior.

Ethics Management in the Workplace

1. *Society.* Improving society could lead to better working conditions, shorter working hours, better treatment of women, children, and employees with disabilities, antitrust laws, regulation of trade unions and business people, government intervention, a healthier environment, etc.

2. *Ethics and turbulence.* The focus on ethics deters people from straying, although it is difficult to alter the basic nature of selfish individuals – consider Bernie Madoff, Conrad Black, and Vincent Lacroix.

3. *Ethics, teamwork, and the bottom line.* Constant communication and open discussions on ethics foster a bond between individuals keen on being ethical and help promote teamwork built on good spirits.

4. *Emotional intelligence and ethics.* Research confirms that emotionally intelligent people are often more ethical than others.

5. *Ethics programs, costs, quality, and public image.* Ethics management programs promote reduced costs related to hiring and firing and treatment of all stakeholders. Still, leaders must set an example by behaving ethically instead of merely preaching about ethics.

Ethics programs promote quality products, services, behavior, a diverse workforce, and fair treatment. Ethics programs also promote a strong public image via demonstrations of integrity and honor in preference to emphasizing the importance of money. Compare the way Johnson & Johnson handled the Tylenol crisis and how McCain dealt with the Maple Leaf Foods crisis with how

(a) Exxon handled the oil spill in Alaska,

(b) BP handled the 2010 Gulf of Mexico Oil Spill, which was the worst in US history,

(c) Toyota handled problems related to their accelerator pedals, electronic systems, and other matters, and

(d) Prominent drug companies in the USA handled research and testing of their drugs on children and animals, marketing practices, overcharging, and false claims, which cost the US government and taxpayers considerable sums of money.

6. *Benefits of ethics management programs.* These benefits include more respect, better teamwork and motivation, and an improved bottom line based on morally sound behavior.

7. *A less stressful life.* A sound ethics management program normally results in more peace of mind and less overall stress.

Ethics Management Programs: An Overview

Business people need practical guidance on establishing, implementing, and observing an effective ethics management program consisting of policies and procedures based on group discussions to guide decisions and behavior. *Employees should be involved in developing an ethics program, and in related training and evaluation, thereby encouraging adherence to the code of ethics.*

As human beings, we all make mistakes, but hopefully, they are not intentional or malicious; this is better than deliberately ignoring the code of ethics. One should help people recognize and address their mistakes while operating ethically.

Ethics Management – Roles, Responsibilities, and Implementation:

1. The CEO should announce the program, champion its cause, and lead by example.

2. An ethics committee at the board level should develop and implement the ethics management program (EMP). The committee should be established to help in implementing the EMP, training and monitoring, and resolving ethical dilemmas.

3. An ethics officer should be appointed to monitor progress and resolve ethical problems/dilemmas.

4. An ombudsperson should be held responsible for ensuring strict adherence to ethical procedures, policies, and practices.

The Code of Ethics

Consider the following guidelines, when developing a code of ethics from the Six Pillars of Character developed by The Josephson Institute of Ethics, USA:

a) Trustworthiness: honesty, integrity, promise-keeping, loyalty;

b) Respect: autonomy, privacy, dignity, courtesy, tolerance, acceptance;

c) Responsibility: accountability, pursuit of excellence;

d) Caring: compassion, consideration, giving, sharing, kindness, loving;

e) Justice and fairness: procedural fairness, impartiality, consistency, equity, equality, due process;

f) Civic virtue and citizenship: law-abiding, community service, and environmental protection.

An organization can be sued for breach of contract if its practices are not in accordance with its policies. Firms must review their policies at least once a year, to ensure that they are in accordance with laws, regulations, and ethical "best practices."

Topics typically addressed by codes of conduct include the dress code; avoiding drugs; being cooperative, reliable, and prompt; maintaining confidentiality; not accepting personal gifts from stakeholders as a result of employment; not discriminating; respecting the rights of other stakeholders; avoiding conflicts of interest; complying with laws; not using the firm's property for personal use; and reporting illegal or questionable activity. Ethics goes far beyond the law.

Ethics Tools: Policies and Procedures

1. Review all personnel policies and procedures with all employees, and obtain their feedback on an ongoing basis. Update policies and procedures, to ensure desirable conduct, while avoiding ethical dilemmas, such as conflicts of interest or infringing upon the rights of stakeholders. Ethical behavior should be rewarded, while unethical behavior should be punished.

2. To demonstrate corporate social responsibility, firms often institute policies and procedures to recycle waste, donate to local charities, pay employees to participate in community events, pay attention to customer needs promptly and in a fair manner, and so on. Ensure that job descriptions and performance appraisals are based on fairness and true appreciation.

3. Ensure that all employees are adequately trained in the ethics management program.

4. A grievance policy is required, to handle disagreements between employees.

5. An ethics hotline must be in place to allow feedback on an anonymous basis.

Ethical Dilemmas

Ethical dilemmas faced by managers are often complex and sometimes without clear-cut guidelines for what is right and what is wrong. Several factors influence decisions, especially in a workplace with a diverse workforce.

Examples of Ethical Dilemmas

(a) If a customer cannot afford our products or services, should we direct him to a suitably priced alternative, which benefits our competitors?

(b) How should we proceed if an employee deserves more money but we cannot afford it?

(c) If we claim to encourage the hiring of minorities, are we justified in disregarding an immigrant on the basis of his very limited command of the English language? Do we hire him and suffer? Do we hire him on condition that he improves the standard of his English within (say) three months, or do we hire him and pay for him to attend English classes?

(d) One of my employees refuses to be trained by a gay person who seems to be attracted to him. What should I do?

(e) My boss has confided in me about the pending layoff of a fellow employee, and I have promised to keep silent on this subject. I know that this employee is planning on buying new furniture. What should I do?"

(f) My boss plans to give a new opportunity (which I am interested in) to a fellow employee, who is supposed to leave soon. What should I do?

(g) Am I allowed to use the company's computer or telephone system for personal reasons?

How to Solve Ethical Dilemmas

Ideally, ethical dilemmas should be resolved by a group within the organization, e.g., an ethics committee comprised of directors, managers, and other staff members. Methods to address ethical dilemmas include procedures, an ethical checklist, and a list of key questions.

The Code of Ethics

The code of ethics cannot possibly be comprehensive enough to cover all situations. Therefore, one's conscience should dictate one's behavior, regardless of the circumstances. *Paying mere lip service to ethics is unacceptable!*

Leaders and managers must realize their vision through people who have been selected based on merit rather than irrelevant criteria, such as friendship or relationships. These people should be trained and motivated through teamwork, caring, sharing, fairness, and respect.

1. *Values.* Leaders must establish their own values and the values of the organization and ensure that employees have similar values through communication and appropriate training.

2. *Trust.* Leaders must facilitate trust between stakeholders and outside parties with a view to promoting effective operations within an ethical framework.

3. *Code of Conduct.* The code of conduct should reflect the ethics and values of the company in question. It should be duly communicated to all stakeholders via literature, training sessions, and other means *on and*

off the job. Ethics and morality go far beyond mere legal compliance. Leaders should communicate with the outside world through words and examples as part of a public relations exercise, which is aimed at boosting corporate image and goodwill. Feedback should be welcomed to help improve effectiveness within an ethical framework.

4. *Act*. To be effective, the entire firm must demonstrate ethical behavior. All unethical behavior must be reported, investigated, and acted on in a fair manner. A concerted effort should be made to recognize and reward exemplary demonstrations of ethical behavior.

5. *Monitor and Sustain Ethical Behavior*. Ethical leadership is mandatory. The organization must gather feedback through surveys, focus groups, one-on-one interviews, and other means to identify stakeholder concerns regarding the presence or absence of an ethical environment. Possible benefits include increased goodwill via improved corporate image, reduced employee and customer turnover, lower legal costs, and more desirable results.

Bernie Madoff, a well-known Wall Street Investment Advisor and one of the founders of the NASDAQ exchange, orchestrated an elaborate fraudulent scheme involving several billion dollars. He was allegedly running a "Ponzi" scheme, mismanaging new funds—amounting to several billion dollars, including the life savings of thousands of his clients—to pay dividends to existing investors. Mr. Madoff was placed under house arrest, with a bail set at $10 million.

A federal judge mandated that a security firm inspect Mr. Madoff and his wife's mail before they left their building and that an inventory of all valuable portable items in his apartment be conducted every two weeks to ensure that he did not try to dispose of them. He was eventually sentenced to 150 years in prison!

Vincent Lacroix, convicted on 200 fraud-related charges totaling more than 100 million US dollars, was sentenced to 17 years and will probably be released in 2025. This scandal is the largest in Canadian financial history.

Numerous other notable examples of fraud exist. The Forbes Magazine "Corporate Scandal Sheet" (Patsurius, 2002) lists, among others, companies like Enron, Time Warner, Bristol Meyers, Halliburton, KMart, Tyco,

WorldCom, and Xerox. This raises the question: Who can you trust?

Enforcing the Code of Ethics

The Sarbanes Oxley Act of 2002, USA, was enacted following the Enron scandal. It aimed to enforce strict reporting requirements and prevent corruption. For some individuals, maintaining ethical standards can be extremely challenging when faced with the temptation of substantial financial rewards and the excitement that corruption may bring.

Noncompliance with the Code of Ethics – The Consequences

Failure to adhere to a strict code of ethics can lead to significant consequences, including the loss of reputation, trust, business, and potential legal ramifications. It is essential always to keep this in mind.

Managers frequently need to pay more attention to the complexity of human rights issues. Their significance is often underestimated. To ensure effectiveness ethically, it is crucial to prevent or minimize violations in this context. The third report to the UN Human Rights Council, which was submitted in late 2008, discusses

a) The government's duty to protect human rights;

b) Corporate responsibility to respect human rights; and

c) The need for greater access by victims to effective remedies.

These core principles have received endorsement from major international business and human rights organizations. Numerous chief executives are staunchly committed to protecting human rights, including healthcare, safe drinking water, decent working conditions, mutual respect, non-discrimination, and global justice. They believe that this commitment fosters goodwill and enhances business performance.

Human rights acts aim to safeguard employees, taking their feelings into consideration. Typically, these acts include grievance procedures for employees who feel exploited. Should a business organization fail to address such issues satisfactorily, the aggrieved employee may seek legal redress and compensation through the courts.

Unfortunately, many business enterprises prioritize their bottom line over ethical conduct. Similarly, numerous individuals hold the view that ethics should remain confined to personal life rather than extend into the business realm. The golden rule to follow is, "Do unto others, as you would have them do unto you." Adhering to a code of ethics might result in short-term financial or other sacrifices, but it is likely to yield significant dividends in the medium and long term.

Practical Emphasis and Approach

How do ethics integrate with organizational goals and employee performance? Several organizations specialize in offering guidance to business enterprises in the realm of ethics, focusing on identifying ethical risks and establishing systems that promote higher standards of business conduct.

Employees who witness ethical leaders demonstrating and promoting honesty, fairness, respect, and trust in the workplace report more positive experiences. Furthermore, these employees are less inclined to compromise on ethics or engage in misconduct at work while also experiencing greater job satisfaction.

Feedback

When developing ethics programs, executives should welcome feedback from other employees, perhaps anonymously (to avoid acts of revenge against the feedback providers), and act on it. The approach should itself be ethical in nature!

An Ethics Program: Introduction and Development

Introducing and developing an effective ethics program requires companywide cooperation, encompassing communication, feedback, and implementation. Leaders must exemplify ethical behavior, leading by action rather than speech alone, in their efforts to satisfy stakeholders.

It is crucial to clearly define ethics and consistently demonstrate ethical behavior that aligns with our ethical beliefs. By respecting employees and treating them as part of the corporate family, they are more likely to adopt ethical practices. This approach enhances the corporate image, attracts quality clients, and helps avoid scandals and negative publicity.

In the business realm, terms like "transparency," "core values," and "going green" are often used. However, ethics extend beyond these catchphrases. The Concise Oxford Dictionary defines ethics as "the science of morals in human conduct." Ethical training should be reinforced by ethical conduct. Merely preaching about the importance of ethics while making false promises, placing unreasonable demands on employees, or offering unpaid internships under the guise of resume-building does not suffice. Although legal, these practices may not be ethically sound.

Many people view certain practices as ethically ambiguous. For example, offering unpaid internships to students who seek work experience is often seen as exploitation. Similarly, the ethicality of stem cell research, especially when it involves destroying a "living being" for "scientific progress," is debated.

Ethical considerations should focus on fairness and integrity. Suggestions for improvement should be constructive and positive, fostering a healthy work environment and community. Corporate scandals involving companies like BP, Toyota, Enron, Arthur Andersen, Pfizer, and individuals like Tiger Woods have eroded trust. Outsourcing jobs to countries with cheap labor, sometimes involving child labor, results from intense competition and a focus on bottom-line results, leading to unethical business practices.

A genuine "green" approach is essential, not merely as a marketing strategy, or a public relations exercise. Specialist consultants can assist businesses in authentically adopting sustainable practices.

Despite the Civil Rights Act of 1964, discrimination based on race, color, religion, sex, national origin, disability, or age persists in America. The Act mandates a "zero tolerance" policy towards such discrimination, whether conscious or unconscious.

Public opinion often influences personal ethics more than legal regulations or a company's code of ethics. The collective voice of many can drive legal changes.

Ethical business and investment focus not only on profit, but also on how it is earned. This perspective encompasses social responsibility, both nationally and internationally, addressing safety, child labor prevention, honesty, fairness in employment and remuneration, environmental issues, health implications, and investment in hazardous products, among other concerns.

Ethics go far beyond the law. Some ethical actions can lead to a change in the law, e.g., where there is pressure from many people to ensure equality for all. Ethical actions are not always legal. Interestingly, the UK Consumer Protection Regulations, 2008, consider it illegal to mislead customers. Before the Act in question, such actions were considered perfectly legal, though unethical!

The flip side of the situation in question: the effects of the ethical decision—is a significant influence on ethical judgment. An ethical decision might not be regarded as sensible, if it benefits some people at the expense of more people, that is, if it is not "for the greater good." This type of argument is frequently used to defend unethical actions and policies.

The Basis for Ethical Decision Making – Fairness

In order to be ethical, one must be objective, fair, and able to see other people's points of view. This is difficult in times of pressure. The following are some guidelines:

1. Be fair – this is more important than boosting your own ego.

2. Ascertain the facts of the situation.

3. Review your previous experience and the experience of others in a similar situation.

4. Appreciate the short, medium, and long-term consequences, of the decision.

5. Be aware of the law related to the matter at hand.

6. Consult people with the required expertise.

7. Ask those who will be affected by the decision, to participate in the decision-making.

Workplace Bullying – Unethical and Professionally Unacceptable!

Bullying is both unethical and professionally unacceptable, as it represents a deliberate and repeated manifestation of uncivilized behavior. This behavior involves manipulation and abuse of power, often for self-gratification, and it progressively undermines a person's mental, emotional, and physical well-being, in an effort to secure an unfair advantage. In the context of schoolyard bullying, the perpetrators are children, and their behavior is overseen by the leaders, namely, the school administration.

However, in the workplace, the situation often differs: the bullies can be the leaders themselves, such as managers and supervisors. In these scenarios, reporting a bully to the HR department, for instance, might inadvertently expose the victim to greater risks of bullying, hindered career progression, or even termination under the pretext of being a "troublemaker!"

Workplace bullying includes:

1. Acts of aggression: assaulting a person or destroying that person's property, verbal abuse, teasing, playing tricks, spreading malicious rumors, half-truths, lies, or gossip;

2. Criticizing a person's lifestyle or habits in an attempt to isolate them socially, weaken their support mechanism, lower their morale, and then bully them;

3. Undermining/impeding a person's work/opinions, setting impossible deadlines, reminding them of their mistakes, taking credit for someone else's job performance;

4. Removing areas of responsibility without cause, or excluding someone from certain projects; threatening job loss, etc., to reduce a person's value to the business enterprise and its top management;

5. Micromanaging an employee, intruding on their privacy by spying on and pestering them, e.g., insisting that the Internet is a corporate resource and that private usage will adversely affect corporate bandwidth. Results-oriented human beings should have access to their cell phones, legitimate websites on the Internet, and their email accounts, during breaks or (say) 15 minutes of company-paid time

during the day; otherwise, the cost of demotivation will far exceed the cost of "adverse bandwidth performance!"

6. Sexual harassment is a form of bullying: abuse of power and disrespect.

Bullying, which can be rooted in race, gender, age, or other attributes, impacts both victims and witnesses, leading to feelings of anger, stress, and a decrease in job satisfaction. This results in diminished effectiveness at work and in other areas, an increase in sick leave and health care costs, reduced employee volunteering, and fewer positive remarks about their employers. Such consequences inevitably affect recruitment efforts and other facets of the company's well-being.

Although employees generally understand what constitutes workplace bullying, only a small fraction of those who have been bullied actually acknowledge experiencing it. According to statistics published by the US-based Workplace Bullying Institute,

~35% of US workers report being bullied at work

~58% of targets are women

~68% of bullying is same-gender harassment

Whereas male bullies pick on men and women, female bullies tend to pick on women more often than they pick on men!

1. **Question:** What are the typical traits of a workplace bully?

Answer: A show of superiority via body language and tone of voice, constant shuffling of paperwork, snacking, walking around and taking excessive breaks to hide their own inefficiency.

    a. Talkers, rather than doers, i.e., those who can't "walk the talk."

    b. Nitpicking, i.e., "majoring in minors," to destroy the self-confidence and morale of the victim and take advantage.

    c. Developing special relationships with key personnel to diffuse opposition to bullying tactics.

2. **Question:** Whom do bullies target?

Answer: Targets include various professionals and nonprofessionals, on an individual or group basis if they are not expected to mount any serious opposition. Bullying is more highly prevalent in blue-collar, male-dominated jobs, where the tendency to report bullying incidents is relatively low, for fear of being branded a coward, i.e., for fear of one's masculinity being "put on trial," so to speak. (The same reasoning prevents some men from reporting the domestic abuse that they are subjected to.)

3. **Question:** Why do bullies get away with bullying?

Answer: Bullies get away with bullying because there are few workplace policies and laws to protect the targets, victims, and witnesses of bullying, except in the case of sexual harassment (which is also a form of bullying: abuse of power and disrespect). Moreover, leaders may not be inclined to discourage results-oriented bullies despite considerable talk about the importance of "business ethics!"

4. **Question:** What can employees do about bullying?

Answer: Employees can collectively diffuse the situation by identifying bullies, isolating them, exposing them, standing up to them, reporting them to the HR department or to their trade union (if relevant), or even enlisting the support of another bully to confront and neutralize this type of behavior. Training sessions can help when combined with a confidential reporting structure, although it is difficult to alter the basic nature of certain individuals, who may need counseling.

Several years ago, during my tenure as a business consultant, there was an incident where a target of bullying, after issuing several warnings, finally punched the bully in the nose. To avoid adverse publicity and a costly lawsuit, the employer covered the resulting medical bill.

A less extreme approach would be for an employee who suffers mental, emotional, or physical injury due to workplace bullying to sue both the company and the abusive employee as joint respondents in the claim. If legal statutes fail to motivate employers to address bullying, the impact of economic realities surely will!

5. **Question:** How can a candidate for a job identify a bully at a job interview?

Answer: The candidate can assess the interviewer's office layout and content, including the chair, desk, walls, etc., and observe his or her mannerisms and tone of voice. It's important to note whether the interviewer maintains eye contact or avoids it when the interviewee makes eye contact. Observing the interviewer's clothing and body language is also crucial. Additionally, consider if the interviewer intentionally left the door open, potentially allowing interruptions, or abruptly ended the interview, possibly depriving the candidate of a job opportunity due to fear of being outperformed. If the candidate has the opportunity to meet other employees, he or she might identify bullies based on these criteria.

Many years ago, during an interview with a company's finance director, I was introduced to the president for my second interview. The president, a tall, slim, balding man in his late fifties, was seated in a dimly lit room on an expensive leather chair, seemingly envisioning himself as a character in "The Godfather." He inquired about my areas of expertise beyond accounting. I mentioned that I had recently written a book on business and was seeking a publisher. His response was skeptical, questioning the book's relevance and the value of many business books.

I retorted, "This book is aimed at those who have spent 25 years in the same chair, gazing at their receding hairline in the mirror and boasting, 'I have 25 years of experience'." This comment visibly angered him. However, he soon calmed down, and I was offered the position of assistant finance director. I declined the offer, as I would be uncomfortable in an unethical work environment.

6. **Question:** What questions can candidates ask, and what clues should they look for at a job interview?

Answer: Candidates should thoroughly review the company's website, primarily designed for promoting the company, to learn about its products, services, board of directors, and managers. It's crucial to check whether women are (almost) equally represented in these areas and to seek clarification on any ambiguous matters. I recall working for an organization with a board of directors comprising several men and one inefficient woman, included merely to give the impression of the company's belief in "equal opportunities for women" – a farcical situation! Candidates must inquire about the corporate culture during interviews: is it friendly and caring? It's important to maintain eye contact, paying attention to the interviewer's tone of voice and body language, to gauge the veracity of their statements. Endeavor to understand the job responsibilities and the company's hiring policies, such as whether there's a preference for internal promotions and the effectiveness of the HR department.

In the US, while bullying is acknowledged as harmful to occupational health, there is minimal political or corporate initiative to curb it. Discrimination laws encompass race, sex, religion, age, disability, sexual orientation, and harassment. Additionally, workplace safety and union protection laws allow employees to litigate on the basis of "a hostile environment."

In Canada, provinces like Ontario (with Bill 168: the workplace harassment and violence legislation), Quebec, and Saskatchewan have implemented legislation concerning health and occupational safety, which includes workplace bullying.

In the UK, bullying is tackled through laws related to harassment and contractual law. This includes employment contract laws based on good faith, trust, and confidence between the contracting parties. These laws permit an employee to terminate their employment contract on grounds of constructive dismissal and seek damages (in bullying situations.) Case law:

a) Majrowski v Guy's & St Thomas' NHS Trust (UK) [47], wherein an employer was held liable for one employee's harassment of another and

b) Green v DB Group Services (UK) Ltd [48], wherein a bullied worker was awarded > £800,000 in damages. Where a person is bullied on the grounds of sex, race, or disability, antidiscrimination laws apply.

In Ireland, the Safety, Health, and Welfare Act of 2005 mandates that both companies and employees take necessary actions to prevent workplace bullying, with serious consequences for noncompliance.

In Spain, bullying falls under the category of labor harassment, acknowledging its impact on the work environment.

In Sweden, the Ordinance of the Swedish National Board of Occupational Safety and Health places significant pressure on employers and employees to prevent workplace victimization.

Meanwhile, in Australia, workplace bullying is commonly linked with laws concerning workplace harassment and safety, with each state having its own specific legislation.

Conclusion

Compliance with ethical standards offers several benefits, such as heightened loyalty among customers, attracting higher quality employees, and reduced employee turnover, which stems from increased job satisfaction and lower stress levels. Additionally, adherence to ethical standards leads to a larger pool of investors, an enhanced corporate image, and increased goodwill, contingent upon the public's awareness of the company's commitment to ethical practices. The UK Institute of Business Ethics proposes a straightforward test for ethical decision-making in the business realm. This test involves asking oneself the following questions and being able to answer "yes" to each of them:

1. Transparency: Am I willing to inform the concerned parties of my decision?

2. Effect: Have I tried to minimize the harmful effects of my decision?

3. Fairness: Would those affected by my decision consider it fair?

CHAPTER 3 – Anger Management: The Road to Salvation?

Anger is a normal human emotion that must be controlled! Failure to control anger can lead to problems that could affect the overall quality of one's life.

The Nature of Anger

Anger is "an emotional state that varies in intensity, from mild irritation to intense fury and rage," according to Charles Spielberger, Ph.D., a psychologist specializing in studying anger. It is accompanied by physiological and biological changes: your heart rate and blood pressure go up, as do the levels of your energy hormones, adrenaline, and noradrenaline. You could be angry at a person, such as a coworker, or an event, such as a traffic jam or a canceled flight, or on recalling traumatic or enraging events. One could argue that a certain amount of anger is necessary for survival. As outlined below, anger can be dealt with by expressing, suppressing, or calming.

(a) Expressing your feelings in an assertive manner (i.e., being respectful of yourself and others) rather than being aggressive (i.e., pushy or demanding) is preferable when expressing anger. Be precise about your needs and how they can be satisfied, without hurting others.

(b) Suppressing your feelings and converting or redirecting them, by focusing on positive and constructive aspects, while bearing in mind that unexpressed anger can cause high blood pressure, depression, vengefulness, cynicism, or hostility. People who are constantly criticizing others and being cynical may suffer from unsuccessful relationships, and counseling may be advisable in such cases.

(c) Calming down, i.e., controlling your outward behavior and your internal responses, and taking steps to lower your heart rate.

As Dr. Spielberger notes, "when none of these three techniques work, someone will get hurt."

Anger Management, Emotions, and Arousal

Anger management aims to reduce the emotions and physiological arousal caused by anger. Some people get angry more easily and/or intensely than others and may become destructive or withdraw socially, sulk, or become irritable when faced with an unjust situation. The cause of anger may be genetic, physiological, or sociocultural. Some children are irritable from an early age. Many of us believe that it's alright to express anxiety, depression, or other emotions but not anger. As a result, we may not learn how to handle anger constructively. Typically, people who are easily angered come from families that are ineffective at emotional communication.

Expressing Anger

Expressing anger may actually aggravate an existing situation. Try focusing on the root cause of anger and work towards eliminating it.

Dealing with Anger

Relaxation

Deep breathing, relaxing imagery, yoga, and other forms of meditation can help calm a person down, as can additional leisure time, entertainment, sightseeing, and holidays.

Cognitive Restructuring

Angry people often overreact and aggravate a situation by stressing other individuals out and alienating them. People who are easily angered tend to be disappointed, frustrated, and hurt when things get tough. In extreme cases, you may need to handle the problem or its cause, instead of focusing on the solution, pending "divine intervention."

Better Communication

Listen carefully and ascertain the cause(s) of anger, e.g., you like more freedom and personal space, but your partner wants more closeness. If he or she starts complaining, do not retaliate by criticizing your partner; otherwise, the latter may feel neglected or unloved.

Humor and its Impact

Humor can defuse rage but should not offend anyone. When you get angry and refer to people in a strange manner, try to imagine what you are saying. If you think of a coworker as a bag full of garbage, picture the latter sitting at his or her desk. When you feel that things ought to go your way, picture yourself as the king of the whole wide world: an individual to whom everyone is always answerable, regardless of the circumstances! Then, you will (probably) realize that you are being unreasonable.

Changing Your Environment, Lifestyle, Diet, and the Need for Adequate Sleep

Immediate surroundings, problems, lifestyle, a low level of intimacy, responsibilities, the quest for perfection, and your current diet can induce anger. Always ensure adequate sleep, personal time, and space for times of the day that are particularly stressful. For example, when you come home from work, you may wish to be left alone for several minutes, barring emergencies. This would make you more effective in life.

Controlling Your Anger: Some More Tips

Timing: If you are generally tired at night, try discussing important matters at other times.

Avoidance: If any room in your house is messy, shut the door instead of getting upset.

Finding alternatives: If your daily commute through traffic leaves you in a state of rage, map out a less congested route or more scenic route, or opt for public transportation.

Being assertive: Angry people need to be assertive rather than aggressive. You cannot eliminate anger, frustration, pain, loss, and the unpredictable actions of others, but you can change how you let such events affect you, thus increasing your happiness. You can be polite and in control of your emotions instead of going overboard.

Ethics, Legal Implications, Public Image, and Other Matters

Public displays of anger can have legal implications, as in the cases of Naomi Campbell and Russell Crowe. The former, a renowned model and notorious character, is well-known for her temper tantrums, outbursts of anger, and shenanigans. Her way of dealing with this problem is by looking at the gloves she wore when working as a New York City sanitation worker as part of her punishment for assaulting her former maid, Ana Scolavino.

Russell Crowe, a Hollywood bad boy, was arrested in New York in 2005 on charges of assault and possession of a weapon for (allegedly) throwing a telephone that struck a hotel employee in the face. Crowe confessed that he "was upset because he couldn't get a call out to (his wife in) Australia," but subsequently claimed that jet lag, his disappointment over *Cinderella Man,* and separation from his family aggravated his response, thereby failing to accept full responsibility, for the incident. Later on, when interviewed by David Letterman, he publicly apologized to the hotel employee and paid him a six-figure settlement, possibly to avoid a civil lawsuit.

Crowe threw in a humorous twist at one of his rock concert performances by displaying a golden replica of the telephone in question. Also, while hosting the Australian Film Industry Awards, Crowe showed the audience an old-fashioned telephone and added, "If there are any problems, and you do get up here and go on too long, then (say) 'hello' to my little friend."

While performing in a play in Australia, Crowe head-butted a fellow actor for screaming at him and calling him names. He explained that his colleagues tried to restrain him by holding his arms and that his head was, therefore, "all I had left to hit him with, and he f deserved it." Crowe believes that anger is a prerequisite for survival and that "… holding and suppressing (anger) is … bull."

In 1999, two individuals were accused of blackmailing Crowe on the basis of a security video that showed the actor fighting with a man and arguing with a woman outside a nightclub in Coffs Harbor, Australia. They were subsequently freed on the grounds of insufficient evidence.

Conclusion

The world seems to abound with anger. Problems associated with defiant children and domestic violence are at critical levels worldwide. Some minors are being excluded from schools because of public outbursts of anger and violence towards teachers, fellow students, and school property. Corporate performance is being undermined by stress and violence in the workplace. These issues must be addressed promptly; otherwise, there will be dire consequences!

CHAPTER 4 – The Customer: The King of All He Surveys, or Merely an Enigma?

The success of a business, which is often gauged by profitable growth, depends on its leadership, the management of the business enterprise, and the satisfaction of all its stakeholders: owners, directors, managers, other employees, customers, suppliers, the community, the government, and related parties. In this chapter, we shall confine ourselves to discussing the significance of customers. A satisfied customer is like a tree that bears good fruit for the business. Therefore, organizations must work towards satisfying customers (though not at the risk of harming other stakeholders) and building trust. Where customers provide feedback, they act as independent consultants offering advice free of charge.

The Customer – Is He (or She) Always Right?

Customers are the lifeblood of a business enterprise; their satisfaction is a primary objective, in most circumstances. Sometimes, it helps to ask the customer,

"What can I do to make you feel better?" In rare situations where it seems impossible to satisfy a customer, one is advised to throw in the towel and move on tactfully because the welfare of employees, and other stakeholders, should not be sacrificed, for the sake of the customer! The old saying, "The customer is always right," is, in my opinion, not applicable everywhere *because leaders must take care of all stakeholders rather than just customers alone!*

On our bad days, we are capable of behaving inappropriately. As human beings, we have our limitations, and we sometimes regret how we acted on certain occasions. Some of us get a chance to apologize and patch up our relationships, while others do not. Some of us suffer from too much stress and have an anger management problem, which calls for counseling. The foregoing should be borne in mind when dealing with demanding customers.

Disappointed customers are those whose expectations have not been met. Listen carefully to the customer's words and observe the tone of voice and body language to thoroughly understand the problem. Try to solve the problem during your interaction with the customer: do not wait until you lose the customer (and related referrals) to figure out what went wrong!

Sometimes, a customer may complain about a product or service and may wish to cancel the sale. Listen carefully to the reason(s) for the customer's disappointment, summarize (your understanding of) the problem, and get the customer's confirmation of your interpretation, thereby showing the customer that you care about him or her. This builds trust between you and the customer. Before offering a win-win solution, encourage the customer to propose a solution while ensuring that you stay calm and focused on the corporate objective.

Never mislead a customer regarding a product, service, warranty, corporate policy, or any other matter. An unethical approach shows a lack of respect and will probably cost you in the short, medium, and long term!

Ensure that your sales force is well trained, polite, friendly, honest, caring, curious to find out what the customer wants, and willing to probe sufficiently to satisfy him or her. Salespeople should adopt a positive approach that focuses on a win-win solution. In cases where the salesperson cannot satisfy the customer's wants, the salesperson should suggest suitable alternatives based on probing.

Always thank the customer, regardless of whether or not you make a sale or solve his or her problem. If you have wronged the customer, apologize instead of "bluffing your way," and be sure to provide speedy and fair solutions that reduce his or her stress level.

Most companies aim to achieve profitable growth. Profitable growth flows from a satisfied and growing customer (and stakeholder) base through referrals and repeat business, coupled with creative management, a motivated workforce, and innovation. Profitable growth should never be taken for granted. There was a time when people would rush to movie theatres, but in the last decade or so, many people have held back, preferring to wait until the movie is shown (a few months later) on a pay-per-view channel at a fraction of the cost of a cinema ticket. Others prefer to buy a DVD copy of the movie, whether it's the original copy or (as is sadly common now) a pirated version, which is often available within two weeks of the release of the film in question. The movie can then be watched in the comfort of one's own home. As a result of this change in attitude, movie theatre owners have lost a considerable amount of business, and some have been forced to close down. Movie theatre owners took profitable growth for granted and failed to envision such a dramatic change in the attitude of moviegoers!

In 2003, Fred Reichheld published an article in the *Harvard Business Review* demonstrating a significant correlation between customer referrals and corporate growth. Together with Satmetrix, an established company, Reichheld used this knowledge to establish the Net Promoter™ score, which refers to the number of promoters minus the number of detractors within a customer base. Promoters are happy customers who refer your products to others, while detractors are dissatisfied customers who are neutral or on the verge of defecting. According to Reichheld, tracking and monitoring this crucial metric, is the best way to outperform competitors. One must develop more promoters than detractors and motivate all employees to focus on customer satisfaction.

There is often a lag between the first negative experience with a customer and its impact on the overall relationship. During that lag, customer service personnel can prevent any further damage via remedial action. Developing customer referrals, through promoters, is the most effective way of growing profitably.

Successful Customer Experience Management (CEM) programs result from multiyear commitments, from the CEO to the lowest paid employee and subcontractor of the company, on a regular and frequent basis, with adequate support from the sales department. The costs and benefits of CEM should be compared. The customer experience data received must be relevant and actionable, and the CEM program must be consistent with key corporate metrics and incentives; for example, the bonus plan needs to be in sync with CEM program goals.

Sharing of Information with Employees

An effective CEM program calls for sharing customer experience data among all related employees, as well as the best practices that arise during the program's life once these practices have been identified. CEM calls for customer interaction, memory jogging notes and due action and is extremely effective in steering the company towards profitable growth if implemented with care and passion, accompanied by due motivation. Mere statistics do not confirm the existence of an effective CEM program!

The CEM program must ensure that the right people always have access to the right data in a timely manner. Constraints include the quality of the sample of customers chosen (and opting) for feedback and action and their willingness to reply promptly. Employees should respond quickly and effectively; otherwise, they will lose customers and their referrals.

Customers should envision their suppliers as a holistic organization, that consists of several touchpoints rather than a series of unrelated departments. Customer behavior is influenced by customer experience with suppliers. Favorable experiences lead to high customer retention, referrals, and profitable growth.

The Internet and immediate customer satisfaction surveys, enable the receipt of customer feedback, within a short period.

If your actions follow suit, advertising your commitment to customer satisfaction, can be a great way to attract new customers. In short, "practice what you preach," in an ethical manner. The key to success lies in having customer experience data and an actionable plan. Companies must blend new capabilities with the old standards in the following ways:

1. Understand and Appreciate the Data: Effect changes in business policies and procedures in line with customer data.

2. Evaluate Customer Needs: Pick areas that need improvement and act upon them.

3. Redesign the Process: You may have to redesign the processes/steps related to the customer experience. Liaise with your customers, product managers, and IT department to ensure a thorough understanding of the customer experience. Define success and ROI metrics during the redesign process to ensure the accuracy of subsequent measurements.

4. Deliver a New Experience: Initiate a pilot program to be completed in less than three months and proceed carefully. Demonstrate success successively, in line with success metrics, and publicize the results on completion. Provide feedback and financial outcome data to senior management to ensure smooth resource allocation and positive customer experiences.

5. Measure: Update the customer file as you gather and act on customer feedback. Study revenue patterns, and establish whether there is an improvement or

deterioration in the bottom line. In other words, identify whether your methods and actions were justified. Customer loyalty is related to your products and services and customer service, before, during, and after selling to them. Consistent excellence in customer service, is of paramount importance!

Customer Complaints and Feedback

Customer complaints constitute feedback that can be converted into opportunities. The eight magic words to diffuse a dissatisfied customer are: "What can we do to make this right?" Listening to the customer carefully might help solve the problem quickly and inexpensively. Do not assume that technology alone will solve the problem!

Educate Your Customers

Explain the benefits and value of the company's products and services precisely. Ensure that customers can easily provide feedback regarding products, services, customer service, and related matters, whether via Google, the website, the telephone system, the newsletter, or any other channel of communication. Follow up for feedback after a sale, and ask for their suggestions to increase the chance of improvement. Ensure that staff are duly trained and up to date in their knowledge and skills on an ongoing basis.

Customers often find it challenging to evaluate intangibles, such as a visit to an accountant, or to ensure that the same standard of service will be provided or subsequently exceeded. There are some grey areas related to customer loyalty to service organizations. Customer satisfaction is always important, as are interpersonal relationships and the costs of switching suppliers.

Many scholars of customer loyalty believe that suppliers of services, rather than tangible goods, have greater scope for building customer loyalty, largely because of the personal element. Some customers will never consider anyone other than their existing supplier(s). Some customers will blacklist certain suppliers.

Customer satisfaction does not always lead to customer loyalty for somewhat unclear reasons. Researchers continue to be puzzled as to which factor(s) guarantee(s) customer loyalty. Many customers are constantly looking for cheaper products, while assuming that quality does not differ between similar products or services. Customers may decide not to switch suppliers because of the time, effort, and related costs involved in ending existing relationships and building new ones (switching costs). Research has confirmed that interpersonal relationships are particularly important in developing customer loyalty towards service providers. In the retail world, where giant stores and franchises are becoming the norm, small business owners can succeed by engaging in more formalized planning, such as sales promotions, and exceeding customer expectations related to quality and service companywide.

Summary

Your CEM program should focus on customers, and dividends will flow. Mere talk about customer satisfaction is not enough to promote profitable growth; appropriate actions should confirm the organization's commitment to customers (and other stakeholders).

CHAPTER 5 – Family Business and Succession Planning

Introduction

The majority of businesses are family-controlled and managed, yet leadership and management books and related courses discount the significance of the "family" component in most companies. Professional advisers to family-owned and operated businesses focus on the technical component of succession (e.g., tax minimization, estate freezes, family trusts, buy-sell agreements, and wealth management), with little attention being paid to the "family" component: family communication, family expectations, family values, family competencies, family dynamics, and related matters.

Research confirms that approximately 70% of family businesses will not survive into the 2nd generation, and 90% will not make it to the 3rd generation, primarily because of family-based rather than business-based issues. Succession issues involve transitioning the management and ownership of the business to the next generation of family members through the application of family business best practices.

This should be handled with the current owners and the active family members, while informing the broader family of the outcomes. The trusted advisers should facilitate the process through appropriate advice and monitoring.

The Family Component

The "Three Circle Model" outlined below illustrates the impact of the family component on the management and ownership of family businesses. The "ownership" circle represents the impact of the owners on the family and on the management of the business. The "management" circle represents the impact of management on the family and the ownership. Likewise, The "family" circle represents the impact of the family on the management and ownership. The first two circles are common to all businesses, but the family circle is unique to family businesses.

The conventional Three Circle Model shows that the family circle has a significant impact on the management and ownership of the business, with the latter functions typically vested in the family. Therefore, the ability of family businesses to outperform their nonfamily counterparts and successfully transfer the business to the next generations depends on their ability to manage the family component of the business.

Family businesses can benefit innumerably to family members, nonfamily employees, and their communities. Family members in business tend to demonstrate a greater sense of passion, loyalty, and commitment to each other and to the business. Family businesses favor passing ownership to the next generation of family members, thus providing further motivation to perform beyond expectations. Problems include the possibility of conflicting goals, values, personalities, expectations, work ethics, choice of employees, compensation packages, lack of formal planning, and related matters.

The challenges of family business include:

1. Resolving conflicts among family members in the business;

2. Formulating a succession plan;

3. Developing a strategic business plan;

4. Developing a retirement and estate plan.

Family Business Best Practices

Family-owned and operated businesses need customized solutions, for effective management of the family component based on existing best family business practices. Identifying what needs to be done, when, by whom, and how can be daunting for the family business. Family business practitioners understand all three circles – ownership, management, and family – and how they interrelate. They can help family businesses manage the all-important family component during the succession process.

Succession Processes and Activities

The family business succession plan comprises the management and ownership succession processes, each with its own set of activities. The management succession process should precede the ownership succession process, and the latter must support the former. There are several activities, to integrate family members into the management and ownership succession processes and to make them feel comfortable regarding their future.

Family business meetings (FBMs) for the active family members, family council meetings (FCMs) for the broader family, and family business rules help guide the succession process, the effective management of the family component, the grooming of successors, and the integration of the active family members into key management activities. The ownership succession process comprises the same channels of communication (FBMs, FCMs, and the family rules) as in the management succession process, but different types of succession issues are discussed.

Desired Outcomes

The current owners must be comfortable with the management and ownership succession plans and with the necessary assurances regarding skills, commitment, and values because of their investment in the business. The next generation of owners must be comfortable with the proposed roles and responsibilities of the management succession team, the compensation philosophy, the distribution of wealth, and the funding of the ownership transition; otherwise, they may delay the implementation of the succession plan.

The current owners should approve the succession strategies and provide both parties with the necessary comfort levels to implement them. In order to manage the family component of the management succession process, the business should consider the following:

1. Who is to lead the management succession process;

    1. Communication through FBMs (active family members only), FCMs (the broader family members), and family business rules (guidelines/policies/rules to guide the succession processes);

    2. Family members as managers: training, compensation, and performance reviews;

    3. The role of family members in business planning; and

    4. The role of family business practitioners.

Management must state where the business is headed and how it will get there. Everyone must understand the company's goals and strive for their achievement, bearing in mind the family component.

Communicate! Communicate! Communicate!

Many family businesses fail, because of a lack of effective communication among family members. Family business meetings and family council meetings enable sound communication.

Family Business Meetings (FBMs) versus Family Council Meetings (FCMs)

FBMs involve *only* family members who are *active* in the day-to-day running of the business. FCMs involve *all* family members who have a stake in the business. The same topics may surface at both types of meetings, but the players are different, the setting and process are different, and the desired outcomes are subsequently different. They should move into a family council setting if the family can hold effective family business meetings.

FBMs should address the family component and its bearing on the management and ownership succession without replacing regular business or board meetings. All active family members need to know who will make specific decisions and how, in order to clarify roles. Other family members or nonfamily members (i.e., employees and advisers) *can* be invited to these meetings, if beneficial to the outcome.

A comfortable setting and initial agenda items that are non-threatening, non-confrontational, and not overly sensitive will give the meetings a fair chance to prove their value. It may take several meetings before participants become comfortable with the format, the agenda items, and each other. Investing time and energy is imperative to get this step right: a poor start should not be allowed to derail the family business meetings. Regroup, hire a facilitator, and then try again.

Personalities

Some personalities are more aggressive, some more analytical, and others more focused on interpersonal relations. Some are risk takers; others are risk averse. Some personalities may clash and cause stressful disruptions within the business. Family members need to make a concerted effort to handle this problem.

Setting up the Family Business Meetings (FBMs)

The owners should assign an active family member to coordinate the time and place of the meeting, frequency, rules, issues to be discussed, recording of minutes, and other matters. It is also necessary to assign someone to chair the FBMs, and it is well worth considering the benefits of using an outside family business practitioner to facilitate these meetings, especially the first few. The role of the FBMs, the management meetings, and shareholder/owner meetings is to make day-to-day business decisions and decisions on succession issues, and develop principles, policies, or rules to guide succession.

These latter are referred to as the family business code of conduct, family creed, family charter, or family business rules to help guide active family members, prevent or solve problems, and reduce conflict. These rules are generally divided into three categories: general, management succession, and ownership succession.

Developing your family business rules with the active family members and reviewing them with the broader family will allow *all* family members to make informed decisions regarding their future in the family business. Many of these issues may have to be tabled more than once so that each active family member has an opportunity to listen, understand, and discuss them, with implications for the management and ownership of the business. The outcomes of these meetings should be summarized in writing for future reference. *Making a commitment to the family business meetings and the development of 'family business rules, addresses the #1 challenge in family business succession: communication, or the lack thereof!*

Ownership succession issues will impact the management succession plan and must be addressed at FBMs. The discussion and outcomes will allow active family members to make informed decisions regarding their future in the business while outlining expectations. Sharing the outcomes with the broader family will inform them of the rules regarding the management succession process and what is being considered.

The management succession timeline will provide the planning horizon for the grooming of successors, who can acquire some of the requisite business skills and knowledge from the current (experienced) owners. The grooming plans are reviewed by the successor group and presented to the owners for review and approval. Upon transition, these plans and the roles and responsibilities of the current owners should meet the owners' expectations regarding the future management of the business while enabling a smooth transition of control to the next generation.

Family Council Meetings (FCMs)

Family councils comprise the broader family: spouses, in-laws, children, grandparents, and grandchildren in the family business. These meetings are held annually every couple of years or more frequently if the business is in a succession/transfer mode. The meetings should focus on informing family members of the "big picture," rather than day-to-day issues and obtaining feedback on family- and business-based issues.

Setting up the Family Council

The family business owners should assign an active family member (or a non-active member with an active member as an assistant) to be the meeting coordinator or chairperson of the family council meetings, with rotation of the role among family members. This member will have access to business information that interests the broader family and may need help in this role.

FCMs usually follow FBMs, wherein the tabled issues will have been discussed. The first FCMs may include a brief history of the family business as a starting point. The participants must know what is expected of them while being informed of how the business is doing, where it is headed, and the role of the family in it.

Performance Reviews

Performance reviews should be an ongoing activity, and family members should be objective in their evaluations. Stress in family relationships may be unfairly reflected in job evaluations. Nonfamily employees may be reluctant to provide negative reviews of family members.

Compensation for Family Members

Developing a compensation strategy for a family business can be challenging. Still, it must be fair and representative of the value of work performed and a top priority item for one of your family business meetings. Common problems include:

1. Managing Family Disagreements during the Succession Process: All family businesses experience disagreements or conflicts, which should be addressed in a timely manner. A family business practitioner or a trusted unbiased third party can effectively mediate and find common ground and resolution. Agreeing to a conflict resolution process is an important part of the family business rules.

2. Integrating the Family Component in Business Planning: Planning tends to be dominated by the owner(s), with little input from children (for fear of being disrespectful) and other members of management or outside advisers. This has often been cited as one of the major stumbling blocks in the management of multi-generational family business enterprises.

Making Use of Outside Expertise

Most family businesses will retain the services of professional advisers, such as accountants, lawyers, bankers, and insurance agents, to assist the business as it evolves. Family businesses should also contact family business practitioners to assist them with their family business succession process: succession planning, strategic planning, and human resource management, while managing the impact of the family component on each of these business processes.

Management succession should precede the ownership succession process/plan. The details on how to manage family communication (family business meetings, family council meetings, and family business rules) and how to groom successors are outlined in the previous section as part of the management succession activities.

Taking the Lead

As in the management succession process, the next generation of owners should take the lead, in the ownership succession process, by formulating the management and ownership succession strategies in consultation with, and with approval from, the owners to provide both parties with the level of comfort needed, to implement succession plans.

Working through the succession plan between the owners and their trusted advisers, without the family's active participation, often leads to unnecessary conflict. Regardless of who leads the process, it must be started. If you have next-generation family members working full-time, in senior management positions, it's time to begin the succession process.

Emotions and Their Impact

Transferring the ownership of any company can create a variety of emotions, ranging from guilt to freedom and happiness. The likelihood of a smooth transition will be significantly enhanced by family business meetings and family council meetings to address succession issues in line with "generally accepted family business best practices." These meetings help manage family members' expectations while enabling them to make informed decisions about their future and providing sufficient comfort to implement the succession plans.

Ownership Succession Issues

The ownership succession issues to be addressed in your family business meetings include the following (also refer to the list of management succession issues in the previous section):

1. How will the family handle communication during this process (family business, council meetings, and family business rules)?

2. What is the current thinking regarding the timeline for the ownership transition? Will it be a gradual transition? If so, when will it start, and when will it be completed?

3. Who can own shares in the family business and why (active family members, non-active members, key employees, next-generation family members who may be interested in joining the business at a later date)? Which scenarios would give the current owners the most comfort? Which scenarios would provide the next generation with the most comfort?

4. How will the ownership transfer be funded? Will future owners be expected to invest personally in

acquiring ownership through (for example) an upfront lump sum payment? Are the current owners willing to have their value in the business paid, in instalments, through the company's profits? What kind of assurances or collateral will the current owners need?

5. What will be the compensation arrangement for the owners, after the transition? Will it be part of the transition price, or will it be separate? How will it be determined?

6. What will be the compensation arrangement for the new owners? Will all of them be paid fair market value for the function each performs? Will bonuses be allocated equally based on ownership or performance or as a percentage of salary?

7. What role, if any, will the current owners play during and after the transition process?

8. At what stage of the ownership succession process will you communicate with the broader family and the employees, to what extent, and who will lead the communication process?

9. What will happen if an owner (current or future) becomes incapacitated, dies, or voluntarily decides to leave or retire from the ownership ranks of the business? What is the exit strategy?

10. What are the criteria for next-generation family members becoming owners? Who will determine the criteria and whether they have been met?

11. Do the owners have a current shareholders' agreement that reflects and supports the succession objectives/plan?

12. Do family members' wills (estate plans) support the succession plan?

13. Would a board of advisers benefit the next-generation owners?

The above ownership issues are best dealt with in the family business meetings with the active members by introducing family business rules (which are then presented to the broader family at family council meetings) to guide the family members in the succession process. These meetings are the primary communication channels in the management of the family component during the succession process.

Governing the Family Component

Governance can be defined as the organizational structures that outline reporting responsibilities, combined with the organizational processes that determine how decisions are made. Corporate governance can include a board of directors and executive management committees with decision-making processes, such as board policies and operational manuals. Family businesses need to account for the family component through family business meetings and councils and use the family business rules for decision-making. Some large family businesses have established a "Family Office" to manage/govern their philanthropic activities.

Family businesses can have a board of directors or a board of advisers. A board of directors (BOD) has legal status and is responsible for overseeing the behavior and performance of the business. Incorporated businesses must hold, at least, an annual BOD meeting. Some family businesses will have a majority of nonfamily members on their BOD.

Unlike a board of directors, an advisory board has no legal status, formal power or legal liability for its actions. This board consists of a group of respected peers selected by the family business to offer advice on a number of business issues, including business strategy, executive compensation, and succession. Such a board can ensure a healthy, long-lived family business that will remain true to its mission and family values.

Minority Shareholders: Managing Expectations

Managing minority shareholders' expectations will help ensure family and business harmony. If the minority shareholders are active family members, they can discuss their expectations at business meetings. If not, this should be one of the agenda items for the family business meetings to be shared subsequently at family council meetings and incorporated in a written policy on the management of minority shareholders' expectations.

Shareholders' Agreement

An integral part of the succession plan is a shareholders' agreement, which formalizes the management and ownership succession plans and decisions made by the active family members during family business meetings. Family business rules developed during the succession process can be embodied or referenced in the shareholders' agreement after working through the succession activities since most of the issues will already have been decided.

Succession Self-Assessment Checklist

To help gauge succession readiness, review the self-assessment checklist below. (Bear in mind that family dynamics and family attributes vary between families and generations.)

1. *Creating a legacy*: Is it necessary to you and to the next generation that the business stays within the family?

2. *Timing*: Have you established a timeline for the management and ownership succession processes? When should the process be started, and should the

next generation of leaders and owners be in place? Has this been communicated to the next generation and the broader family?

3. *Comfort level*: Family issues and/or business issues will impact the future management and ownership of the business. As an owner and parent, are you doing anything to increase your comfort levels and minimize any potential negative impact on the family and the business?

4. *Options*: Are you aware of your options? Do you know where to get the relevant information on the (identified) options so that you and the next generation of managers/owners can make informed decisions about your individual and collective futures in the family business?

5. *Communication*: Communication is the most critical aspect of a successful transition. Decisions should be based on opinions expressed by those affected by the succession process. Do you have a dedicated forum (i.e., family *business* meetings and family *council* meetings) that deals with succession issues and the succession process? Is there an active senior family

member who is well-suited to lead these meetings, and have you considered using an outside family business practitioner for this purpose?

6. *Expectations*: Can you clearly verbalize the expectations of your family members, regarding their future roles/interests in the family business? How did you obtain this information?

7. *Guiding principles*: There are several options when transferring the management and ownership of a family business. Agreeing on some basics will help steer the process and manage family members' expectations. A formal process to discuss management and ownership succession issues (i.e., family *business* meetings) that result in agreed-upon succession principles can pave the way. Have you reflected on your guiding principles and discussed these with the active family members and the broader family? Consider the following:

   • Employment: What are the criteria for the employment of family members? Can spouses and in-laws work in the business?

- Who can own: Will ownership be made available to non-active family members? If so, why, and what are their rights and expectations as non-active family owners? How will the active family members manage this issue (e.g., voting control)? Can spouses and in-laws become owners?

- Compensation: What is your current thinking regarding compensation for active family members, and should it reflect market value?

- Leadership: Will there be only one leader (e.g., president), or will co-leadership be entertained (e.g., co-presidents)? How will they be selected?

- Management succession: How do the management and ownership succession plans tie in and support one another? Is the ownership plan conditional on the management succession being in place, or will both plans be transferred simultaneously? Will the ownership be held in trust until the management succession issues are addressed?

8. *Successor(s)*: Have you identified a successor(s)? Has this been communicated to the next generation? Would the latter have selected the same individual(s)? How do you know?

9. *Changing role*: Have you considered the role you want to/should play during and after the management and ownership transition? Does the next generation support this role?

10. *Income security*: Is most of your disposable income tied up in the family business? Do you know how much you would need to draw from the family business after transitioning it to the next generation? Are you concerned about the security of your investment in the business after the transfer, and is this preventing you from moving forward in the succession process?

11. *Who should lead*: Would you prefer that the next generation of managers/owners take the lead while obtaining your advice, support, and approval during the process, or are you willing to take the lead?

12. *Managing conflict*: Is there an agreed-upon process to deal with family conflict? Is it effective and agreed on by family members?

13. *Business strategy*: Is the next generation planning to take the business in the same direction that you would (growth, profits, and investments)? Has the next generation demonstrated its ability to do so?

14. *Exit strategy*: Will the shareholders' agreement for the next-generation owners include an exit strategy that is considered fair and amicable to all parties while safeguarding the financial viability of the family business? Will it address incapacity, death, and voluntary retirement?

15. *Wills*: Does your will (estate plan) reflect and support your current thinking concerning the future ownership of the family business? Is the next generation aware of this?

16. *Getting started*: Are you having trouble getting started? Can an outside family business adviser assist you in the succession process?

17. *Validation*: Would the next generation be in agreement with your answers to the above questions? How do you know?

Most family businesses do not complete their succession plan.

Sample Family Business Rules

1.Employment of Family Members

The family business owners encourage and support family members' participation in the family business.

- Employment of family members in the family business will be based on opportunity and merit. Compatibility of personalities will also be taken into consideration in assessing the employment and potential ownership of family members.

- Prior to an offer of employment being made to a family member (full or part-time), the offer must be approved by all the owners.

- Family members aspiring to the ranks of management are expected to have the following qualifications:

- University/college degree (or equivalent)

- Three to five years of related work experience outside the family business

- Family members will be compensated based on fair market value.

- A probationary period of six months will be applied to all new family members.

- Family members should preferably report to nonfamily members or to non-direct family members (i.e., not parents or siblings).

2. *Family Members Becoming Owners*

The owners are open to allowing active senior family members to be owners, when they demonstrate their skills and commitment to the family business. For a new family member to enter, approval by the existing owners is required. In such cases, the company will carry out a "freeze": the current value of the company will be determined and distributed among the current owners, in the ratio of their ownership interest, in the form of "freeze" shares (or preferred shares), which the company must pay, as per the agreed on payment terms. At this time, a new class of ownership shares (common shares) will be distributed to the old and new owners. There is no price to pay for these new shares, and subsequent growth of the business accrues equally to each of the owners in proportion to shareholding. This process will be repeated as subsequent owners are accepted into the ownership ranks.

3. *Employment of Spouses and In-laws of Active Family Members*

The employment of spouses and in-laws of active family members in the family business is a delicate and sensitive issue. While not encouraged, this matter will be treated in the same manner as the employment of any family member outlined in policy #1 above.

4. *Executive Compensation*

Executive compensation for family members should be representative of the value of the work being performed; otherwise, it may lead to conflicts.

5. *Exit Strategy*

The shareholders' agreement will provide for a fair and equitable exit strategy from the family business on specific terms and conditions. Otherwise, the terms and conditions will be tabled and approved at a family business meeting and forwarded to legal counsel for future reference.

6. *Retirement Strategy*

In an effort to support the orderly transition of leadership and ownership in the family business among future generations, we propose a mandatory retirement date of 65 unless otherwise agreed to by the rest of the owners.

7. *Minority Shareholders*

The family business commits to informing all shareholders of their roles and responsibilities and what is expected of them. Minority shareholders will be kept informed of ownership-type issues, including periodic business performance results. An annual distribution policy may be formulated.

8. *Conflict Resolution*

The purpose of a policy on conflict resolution is to provide active and non-active family members with a forum to discuss and resolve conflicts related to the family business. Family issues typically impact the business, and business issues usually impact the family.

The owners must establish a conflict management process to address conflicts that are currently having, or have the potential in the future, to negatively impact the business. One of the owners will chair the process.

The chair will schedule a meeting with the appropriate persons and conduct the meeting to facilitate the discussions and find a resolution to the issue.

The chair will consider using an outside facilitator (i.e., an expert in the family business) to assist in dealing with the conflict.

The chair will inform all family members of the existence of the conflict management process and how it operates.

9. *Prenuptial or Nuptial Agreements*:

A prenuptial or nuptial agreement aims to safeguard the ownership/control shares of the family business so that in the event of a marriage breakup, the ownership structure is not inappropriately altered, put at risk, or compromised. Therefore, the following policy is endorsed by the owners.

As a condition of ownership in the family business, the owner is required to conclude a prenuptial or nuptial agreement in a form that is acceptable to the company's corporate solicitor.

Any family member planning to join the ownership ranks of the family business, is encouraged to conclude a prenuptial agreement.

10. *Family Trusts and Other Trusts*

Each owner must ensure, in a form acceptable to the company's corporate lawyer, that his or her family trusts or other trusts support the terms and conditions of the shareholders' agreement with regard to rights and privileges.

11. *Leaves of Absence and Sabbaticals*

There must be a policy regarding leaves of absence and sabbaticals. This will enable family business owners to succeed in their roles as parents, bosses, and owners.

Sabbaticals are intended to accommodate extended leave for the sake of, for example, continued education, health reasons, or exceptional circumstances.

Entitlement is based on working for at least three years in the family business.

The employee's current position, or one comparable to it, will be provided upon return.

The leave is without pay unless otherwise determined by the owners.

If the leave is for educational purposes, costs may be reimbursed upon successfully completing the program.

The approval of all the owners is required.

Leaves of Absence

Leaves of absence are intended to comprise short periods of time (i.e., weeks to months) to allow family members to deal with short-term illnesses or personal issues.

The leave is generally with pay.

Entitlement is based on assessing each individual case, for which the approval of all the owners is required.

12. *Business Loans to Family Members*: Purchasing Goods/Services from Family Members

The family business may experience requests from active and non-active family members for personal loans. These situations can cause long-lasting conflict among the owners and family, if not consistently handled.

All requests for personal business loans or other financial transactions with family members must be approved by a unanimous vote of the owners, with the terms and conditions of the transaction agreed to be confirmed in writing. This would include:

- The total amount of the loan, commitment, or other financial transaction

- Precisely to whom it is being lent or committed

- The proposed payment schedule and any related interest

- What happens in case of default

- Whether the loans should be insured

13. *Philanthropy / Charity*

The family business will develop a strategy for charitable giving to be reviewed and approved by all the owners.

- Which charities do we want to support and why?

- What amount are we prepared to donate annually? This should be budgeted.

- The name in which the funds are being donated (the family business, individuals).

14. *Public Relations*

The owners will decide who will be appointed to represent them in the media and communication with the general public. All requests for written or oral statements by the media or general public, public appearances, and any other public relations activities will be channeled to and handled by the company representative(s).

15. *Conflict of Interest*

Each family member must ensure that he or she is not in a conflict of interest situation while employed in the family business. Any family member who is unsure must table the situation at an executive meeting for review.

A family member employed in the family business will be considered in a conflict of interest situation if he or she has engaged either directly or indirectly, in any related business activities without the consent of the other owners.

A family member who is employed in the family business may not engage in any other active business without the unanimous consent of the owners.

16. *Changes to the Family Business Rules*

Changes to the family business rules require the majority vote, of the active owners. Changes will be presented to the broader family at the next family council meeting.

CHAPTER 6 – How Does One Thrive in a Home-Based Business?

Lack of motivation among employees seems to be a universal problem, resulting from the inadequate leadership and management skills of many leaders, managers, and supervisors, who do not seem to understand that employees are business partners who need to be motivated via ethical leadership: respect, caring, sharing, challenging assignments, etc. A reasonable compensation package, combined with praise, fair criticism, challenging assignments, and other factors, does not guarantee loyalty to the business and low employee turnover!

Many employees, having faced repeated disappointments, feel the need to combat this problem by starting out on their own, with a view to independence, financial freedom, flexible hours, and the freedom to make decisions that could increase their own wealth rather than their boss's. However, frustration with one's boss does not justify starting one's own business, which calls for a great degree of business knowledge and discipline and must be preceded by careful thought and planning, especially in the case of a home-based business. In addition, one needs to be able to set up and control budgets and spending while establishing financial goals and being able to "roll with the punches" when things do not go according to plan. There are times when you will have to work alone, without anyone to talk to or liaise with. Spare time must be used constructively.

Technical expertise alone does not guarantee business success! Many business organizations close down in the early years, thus confirming the need for (ethical) leadership and marketing skills in addition to technical skills. Prior to starting off on one's own, one is advised to attend courses on the leadership, management, and planning aspects of business. In addition, one has to learn from the mistakes of one's former supervisors and managers and treat employees as precious investments in an ethical manner. This will ensure their loyalty while contributing to personal, as well as (profitable) corporate growth.

Before starting out on your own, ensure that you have a set of skills that are in demand and a reasonable amount of cash to tide you over during lean periods of business. Many businesses fail because of a shortage of money for assets or expenses. A line of credit or credit card(s) can come in handy, but you must ensure that the cost of borrowing is justified by the income generated, from usage of the borrowed funds. You must believe in yourself and be positive and persistent. Do not be unduly influenced by tempting advertisements on television, in the press, or elsewhere for products or services that appear to be appealing, cheap, and easy to resell at a profit. Engage in thorough research before embarking on a project or a series of projects.

A home-based business may be geared towards providing supplemental income and eventually replacing one's fulltime job, or it may be an attempt to supplement retirement income if life throws a curve ball during retirement. An action plan based on marketable skills must be accompanied by a willingness to put in a concerted effort to achieve one's goals.

Forming and Naming the Business

If you decide to operate as a sole proprietorship, your liability will be unlimited: if your business assets are insufficient to settle your debts, your creditors can proceed against your personal assets. Adequate insurance policies can protect you, but insurance companies are not really inclined to settle claims in a way that satisfies creditors. Therefore, you can either make up the shortfall or protect yourself from the outset by incorporating (with limited liability) and considering the possibility of closing your corporation and starting a new one, if customers or creditors are unreasonable in their demands.

As far as naming the business is concerned, it is not advisable to use your own name, either because the business enterprise is a separate entity, as distinct from yourself, or because you may wish to sell your business at a future date without selling your name, with implications for goodwill attached to your personal name. Use a name that suits the business operation.

Setting up the Business

Setting up your home-based business will have implications for your privacy and your family life. Communicate with your family members and ensure that you spend quality time with them, giving them their space, adequate telephone usage, and confidentiality regarding the presence of family, friends, neighbors, disturbances, and so on. You must also consider zoning (which you may be able to dispute and ask for a variance, based on your specific circumstances: type of business, low volume of customers, no noise, no environmental hazards, etc.), dedicating space exclusively for business, storage, parking for customers and others, signage, telephone lines, utilities, insurance, tax implications regarding allowable deductions, and other factors.

Establish a healthy relationship with a bank that is known for good service and is geared towards helping businesses, such as yours, while being quite flexible in approach. Ensure that the appropriate licenses are in place to enable you to operate legally and efficiently. You may choose to have a logo that identifies your business and promotes effective advertising.

The Business Plan

A business plan may not be essential to success, but it does help provide a blueprint that can be adjusted if necessary. A business plan outlines the history of the business, its nature and purpose, short, medium, and long-term goals, the target market and characteristics, market research conducted, competitive strategy and related matters. It includes financial statements to show where the business is expected to be headed, over the next (for example) three years.

Operations, Technology, and Related Matters

Some businesses can operate from a corner of a room – others cannot! Be aware of your situation and set up your office accordingly, bearing in mind space requirements, storage, number and frequency of customers, neat appearance of the office and surrounding area, lighting, the floor, furniture, feng shui, hygiene factors, cleaning, mail services, filing, bookshelves, zoning, parking, entrance, greeting customers and related factors.

As far as technology is concerned, ensure that you have good quality telephones, an efficient computer with suitable software, and easy access to the Internet. Technology must be complemented by excellent customer service.

Buying an Existing Business

If you are considering buying a business, be careful when valuing it. Review the financial statements for the past few years, review the credibility of the accountant, and take into account location, market share, growth rate, assets, liabilities, and undisclosed items, such as obsolete inventories or inventories held but not paid for, pending lawsuits, possible goodwill. Ensure that the agreement of sale prevents the current owner from competing with you, for a certain specified period of time and within a certain radius of your location. Interview existing employees and discuss your acquisition plans with them. Distribute questionnaires to ascertain what current employees like and dislike about the company that you are hoping to acquire.

The Importance of a Good Lawyer, Accountant, and Others

A home-based business, like any other business, needs a good lawyer, a good accountant, and a good insurance company for obvious reasons. It also helps to have a healthy relationship with a bank that is quite flexible in its approach. Liability insurance, workers' compensation, business interruption insurance, health, dental, medical, and disability insurance, property insurance, auto insurance, and related matters should also be taken into consideration.

Communication and Business Dealings

You must stay organized and communicate well with insiders and outsiders, such as customers, suppliers, the bank, the government, and others. Be careful in your dealings with people, and also note that you will be busier at certain times of the day. Communication face to face, over the phone, via email messages, and letters, should be courteous and effective. Pay yourself reasonably for the services you provide – *you are not working for your business for free!*

Stay focused and motivated, be creative, attend training courses and business events, join volunteer organizations, and look for lines of business that complement your own business. *Promote yourself at all times, whether you are attending a function or merely visiting a mall, but do not appear to be desperately in need of business.* Your communication skills must impress people so that they want to do business with you. Advertising helps, but it must be complemented by excellent service and follow-up. *People are attracted to successful businessmen rather than those who are depressed and needy – always bear this in mind.*

When you are unproven and starting a business or changing careers, working for free or offering one free service or session may be an effective way of gaining experience and business connections.

CHAPTER 7 – Retirement – A New Haven?

Before retiring, one must live within one's means, e.g., pay off credit card balances within the grace period, eliminate interest charges, buy gas at self-service rather than full-service gas stations, and invest at least 10% of one's income wisely while paying oneself first. Emergency funds are necessary when faced with expenses that are not covered by insurance or to take advantage of excellent bargains.

Consider the impact of the following categories of expenditure that may drain one's financial resources during retirement:

a) Medical expenses due to the age factor;

b) Long-term care expenses, because more women have joined the workforce and are therefore unable to attend to their elderly parents;

c) Heating expenses, unless one will move to a warmer climate, and

d)   Leisure and travel activities.

Possible sources of income during the retirement period include consulting, as a popular form of entrepreneurism, and property management.

Qualified retirement plans include IRAs and Keoghs in the USA, Registered Savings Plans (RSPs) in Canada, and company-sponsored savings programs. Some insurance policies are treated as tax shelters in the sense that certain withdrawals from them are considered to be withdrawals of principal and, therefore, nontaxable. A tax shelter is any investment that enables a taxpayer to claim a deduction, loss, or tax credit that can offset income from other sources. When it comes to investment income from real estate, mutual funds, and other financial instruments, be aware of all the deductions that you are entitled to, and put as much income as possible in the name of the lower-income-earning spouse!

Government benefits and government pension plans can be diminished by postretirement income and assets. In Canada, you may continue to work beyond the age of 65 and avail yourself of unemployment benefits if dismissed in accordance with the rules for employment insurance benefits.

Employee Benefit Plans

Understanding a business enterprise's retirement package may be extremely difficult, but this hurdle must be overcome if one is to benefit from the latter package. The tax implications of such packages, together with incentives for early retirement, should be discussed with one's accountant prior to any decision being taken. Moreover, one has to check the reputation and integrity of the business enterprise in question. Consider the following:

1. Defined Benefit Plans, whereby the firm sets aside money for the employee's retirement based on a formula that takes into account years of service, salary, and other relevant factors. Payment may be in a lump sum or monthly installments, but the tax effects should be considered prior to withdrawal.

2. Defined Contribution Plans, whereby the firm matches the employee's contribution via an agreed percentage or share of profits. Alternatively, the employee may participate in a stock ownership program, whereby the employer matches the employee's purchase of stock at an agreed

percentage. Defined Contribution Plans are portable and normally vest quicker than (1) above; these plans may even be incorporated within (say) a 401K salary reduction program. Beware of small businesses where a few executives receive higher benefits than other employees.

Other Investment Plans

(1) *An individual's house.* An individual's home may provide his main source of security, with some property expenses being tax allowable. Capital Gains Taxes may not be payable upon the sale of the house, depending upon which country an individual lives in. You may consider selling your house and moving to a smaller one, renting an apartment, or taking a mortgage against the equity (i.e., reverse mortgage your house and buying a tax-free annuity, such that the mortgage can be repaid upon the death of both spouses and sale of the house). In Canada, the sale of one's principal residence does not incur any tax liability.

Moreover, real estate can be a good investment if rented to good tenants, with rental income exceeding mortgage payments and maintenance costs. Even if you do not rent out part of your house, your mortgage payments should take into account rent that would otherwise be payable. A 15-year amortization period may be advisable, but make sure to shop around for the best interest rates. Buy at a good price and near water, if possible, with access to transportation, shopping, and schools. You are advised to review *The Smith Manoeuvre*, which can help in wealth creation.

In some cases, it may be cheaper to rent (rather than buy) and invest the difference in mutual funds, for example, to provide a higher retirement income.

(2) *Qualified investment/savings plans* will generate income that is not taxable, but there are penalties for early withdrawal. These plans may incorporate suitable mutual funds. A mutual fund is a professionally managed pool of money. Diversify further by investing in international mutual funds with sound long-term performance records. Mutual fund income is taxable, but the balance can be reinvested. Capital gains are taxable on the disposal of the mutual funds in question, but the formalities involved in encashment may discourage one from reducing one's portfolio of mutual funds.

Government programs may provide a source of income during retirement, but there are specific rules that have to be followed in order to benefit from these.

Life insurance policies can provide a source of income during retirement, but these policies should be considered a last resort, as far as income is concerned, unless one can withdraw cash without tax consequences or one is terminally ill. Life insurance provides financial protection against lost income, debt (including mortgage and taxes), and estate management expenses, including funeral expenses, education, and inflation faced by your loved ones.

Disability insurance policies protect earning power and help cover expenses during disability (own or any occupation, indexed for inflation, waiver of premium, non-cancellable, benefit period after a certain period, percentage of income as disability coverage), and may help an individual retire before the typical age of retirement if he/she cannot work at his own occupation.

Estate Planning

Plan your estate carefully with the help of a suitable financial planner. Joint ownership and children are no substitute for a well-drafted will and an efficient and trustworthy executor. You may need to draft a power of attorney, with the help of a good lawyer, and review your will at specific intervals or as circumstances change. Give a copy of recent wills to an effective lawyer executor, together with a statement of net assets and relevant documents; otherwise, the government will distribute your estate in accordance with the law. A will may have a clause that mentions something like, "any beneficiary who attempts to dispute the contents of this will can and will lose his share of the estate, and this portion will be donated to …. Charity." You may donate to your favorite charity as long as you follow the guidelines set by the tax authorities.

If your heirs are very young, you may set up a trust through an attorney/lawyer to hold property for them, with precise instructions regarding the management of such property.

Proper estate planning will help reduce or eliminate estate taxes, depending on the circumstances. Your estate should be sufficiently liquid to avoid the sale of its assets at knockdown/fire sale prices. Executors should prepare in advance for the task of executing their client's will by discussing with their clients regarding their financial affairs, intentions, location of inventories, records, will, and related matters. Managing the client's estate includes distribution, recordkeeping, filing claims, and related matters.

CHAPTER 8 – Insurance and Other Financial Matters: A Conceptual Approach

Introduction

In this section, we shall look at the subject of life insurance, disability insurance, critical illness insurance, long-term care insurance, mutual funds, segregated funds, retirement, and related matters *(mainly) in a Canadian context*. Needs analysis is of paramount importance.

(a) Living Needs include disability and critical illness coverage, medical, extended health care, long-term care, education for children through RESPS, and (perhaps) Universal Life Insurance policies.

(b) On death, we are concerned with probate and estate taxes, debts (including mortgage and credit cards, loans, etc.), funeral expenses, survivor's income, and the education of children.

Permanent needs include funeral costs, estate taxes, survivor's income, and estate creation for loved ones/charities. Younger people are interested in wealth accumulation; older people are interested in estate protection.

Unilateral Contract: where only one party can change the terms, e.g., face value + utmost good faith + printed contract which cannot be negotiated/altered + aleatory: policy owner knows what the insurance company will do, but the latter does not know what the former will do.

Term Insurance

Term Insurance (usually until age 80) covers temporary risks of a known duration and maybe.

(1) Renewable without a medical examination, but premiums increase in accordance with the schedule of the original policy. It may be cheaper to take a new policy from the same or another company or to be medically examined if one is healthy.

(2) Convertible Insurance can convert to permanent insurance before a specified age, without a medical examination, e.g., if you are uncertain about the future, as in the case of a newly married couple, or

you cannot afford permanent insurance at this point in time. Premiums are based on age.

(3) Nonrenewable insurance requires a new application and medical examination.

(4) Mortgage insurance: no medical + higher premiums, + the policy ends when you sell the house.

Term premium = f (Mortality Cost + Company's Operating Margin + Investment Returns + Tax)

Mortality table: life expectancy based on age, gender, smoking/nonsmoking, and region, e.g., North America.

(Mortality) cost of insurance: Net Amount at Risk x Probability of Death = (e.g.) 100,000 x 0.122%(Mortality Table for Age 30 years)) = 100,000 x 0.122/100 = $122.

Operating margin/policy fee: covers sales commissions, underwriting costs, medicals, rent, salaries, utilities, etc., and profits…say $6 per policy.

Higher Investment Returns mean lower premiums. Each province charges a tax of 6% to insurance companies.

The rating of policies is based on medical conditions (unless diabetes, etc.), smoking, family history, etc.

Term to 100 Policies: a cheap permanent policy when not interested in cash value, e.g., donation. You must pay premiums until the age of 100, and your beneficiary will receive a benefit whether you die before or after reaching the age of 100 years.

Grace Period: if you die during this 31-day period, the beneficiary gets death benefit – o/s premium.

Lapse: If the grace period of 31 days is exceeded, the policy remains dormant for 2 years but can be reinstated upon payment of outstanding premiums + penalties + reinstatement costs + medical examination. The premium is based on the original age but adjusted if the insured person's health deteriorates or if he or she becomes a smoker during the grace/dormant period. The incontestability and suicide exclusion clause starts again, and the company can refuse to reinstate the policy based on factors such as medical conditions.

Incontestability Clause

(a) Nonmaterial Misrepresentation: the insurance company has 2 years (same as for the suicide clause) from the actual policy date to investigate and correct the application.

(b) Material Misrepresentation ≠ *misstatement of age (reduced death benefit)* and the policy can be canceled. If the material misrepresentation is intentional, the company can prosecute, for fraud.

Whole Life Insurance

Whole Life Insurance (WL) covers long-term risks and taxes upon death, and there are insurance as well as investment components, with no premiums being paid beyond the age of 100 years because the investment value should exceed the face value of the policy. Premiums are higher than for Universal Life (UL) policies because investments are more conservative. Adjustable WL has lower premiums than guaranteed WL, but UL is still cheaper.

The owner of the policy can pay more than the stipulated premium and build cash value, which can be used to buy a paid-up policy if and when the owner finds it difficult to pay the stipulated premium. You may choose to buy a limited pay WLI policy and pay for a specified number of years, as guaranteed by the company.

Adjusted cost basis (ACB): Actual Cost of insurance or investment with after-tax dollars = Premiums, the Cost of Pure Insurance, the dividends in par WL policies

Policy Reserve: $ growth within insurance policy.

Insurance proceeds during life: Policy Growth = CSV – ACB is taxable in full as income, whether loan, e.g., 90% x CSV or not ... when you repay the loan, the same excess can be used to reduce taxable income. The unpaid loan and interest will reduce the death benefit.

Insurance proceeds upon death are tax-free to the beneficiary.

Account value: Balance in your account, but the insurance company may deduct a surrender charge.

Owner: The insured may or may not be the life insured but must have an insurable interest: self, spouse, child, stepchild, grandchild, partner, employee, person being funded by Mr. X has an insurable interest in Mr. X or anyone who signs a document stating insurable interest in him or her, subject to company's approval.

Transferring the Ownership of a Policy

If there is a transfer to one's spouse (i.e., lived with him or her for ≥ 12 months or parent of one's child), child, stepchild, grandchild, or parent, then no taxes are payable. The ACB remains the same as that of the original owner.

Other Transfers: tax implications to owner @ Account Value – ACB = taxable income

Transfer to Charity: (i) Donation receipt for CSV of donated policy or (ii) Donation receipt for premiums paid on a donated policy.

Non-forfeiture Benefits

If you do not pay your premiums, they can be paid via an automatic premium loan (APL) through the cash surrender value (CSV). When the CSV runs out, the grace period will begin, and if there is a lapse of more than 31 days, you have to review what was mentioned above. Options include having a Reduced Face Amount of Policy or the CSV can be used to buy a term policy of less than or equal to the original face amount without conversion rights.

Participating Whole Life Policies

Premiums payable may be higher than for non-participating policies. Still, if the insurance company makes a profit, because of reduced costs/higher investment returns, the excess premiums are called policy dividends. These are different from corporate dividends and are used to lower subsequent premiums, invested in accordance with the policy owner's instructions, or to buy an additional paid-up policy or a one year term policy without a medical examination, *depending on the contract.* Such amounts reduce the ACB. If premiums are less than what should have been charged, the insurance company takes the hit.

Universal life insurance policies are flexible or unbundled. The owner can change the face amount, premiums, frequency, and even the life insured, and there is a guaranteed death benefit. The policy reserve of the WL policy is called the investment account of the UL policy and can be used to invest in GICs, stocks, and even mutual funds, *but not in segregated funds.*

Insurance charge = Cost of Insurance as for Term 100 + Policy Fee + Tax;

Insurance Option: level term or Annual Renewable Term (ART) – can be switched to level term within the agreed period;

Grace period = 31 days, with lapse rules as discussed earlier;

Death benefit options: level death benefit/face amount or level death benefit + account value or indexed at agreed percentage or COLA or level death benefit + accumulated gross premiums.

In WL policies, you only receive a level death benefit option.

Withdrawals: excess over ACB is taxable income; e.g., if ACB = $30,000 and Account Value = $40,000, then 75% of the withdrawal is taxable income.

Beneficiaries

The beneficiary will receive the death benefit tax-free, but revocable beneficiaries can be changed, e.g., through a will. If the beneficiary is irrevocable, e.g., owner's estate/other beneficiary, then written consent is needed for any changes, e.g., loans, cashing in the policy, or transfer of ownership.

The death benefit is tax-free and payable in accordance with the owner's instructions (lump sum, installments, annuity, interest only) and is creditor-proof when a beneficiary is named in the policy; otherwise, the death benefit goes to the estate. During life, CSV is creditor proof if the beneficiary is irrevocable or a preferred class beneficiary: spouse, child, stepchild, grandchild, or grandparent.

If the owner and the beneficiary die simultaneously, the latter is considered to have died first, and the death benefit goes to the owner's estate.

Accelerated Death Benefits, Supplementary Benefits and Riders

Living benefits to the life insured: Accelerated Death Benefit (ADB) $\leq$ 50% of the death benefit to the life insured upon terminal illness; critical illness – waiting period $\leq$ 30 days for terminal illness and long-term care when $\geq$ 2 of the following apply: unable to toilet, unable to dress, needs constant supervision, or mentally ill. These benefits per contract will reduce the death benefit.

Disability benefits rider: If disabled per *own* occupation, then the benefit will be paid after 31 days and up to 24 months.

Waiver of Premium: If the life insured is totally disabled per *own* occupation, the insurance company will pay premiums after the elimination period and refund premiums paid during the elimination period, but the Payer Disability rider is applicable for the disability of the owner.

Parent Waiver: When the life insured is a minor.

Dread disease rider: Diseases listed in the policy – the amount paid is deducted from the death benefit, as for a long-term care rider, but different for a critical illness rider.

Term insurance rider: The family coverage rider is applicable, only to the spouse's children between the ages of 14 days and 21 years (or 23 years if studying at an accredited educational institution), even if you do not inform the company of the newborn child. If the life insured dies, the spouse can convert the rider to permanent insurance ≤ 31 days of death.

Guaranteed insurance rider: covers up to 50% of the face amount of the policy and can be bought when offered by the company without a medical examination, but additional insurance will bear a premium according to the age at conversion.

ADD: Double indemnity or twice the face amount of death benefit for accidental death or dismemberment, as defined by the insurance company.

Paid-up additions rider: An extra lump sum payment can expedite the paying up of the policy.

Upon the Death of a Person

Estate: Assets are valued at fair market value (FMV), and liabilities are frozen/crystallized in the estate. No capital gains on the main residence, death benefit, and lottery winnings. Income tax on income to death. RSPs are considered withdrawn and taxable unless rolled over to a spouse, and there is a probate tax @1.5% x estate value.

You must pay taxes to the Canada Revenue Agency, and get a clearance certificate from the latter. Then, the executor pays creditors, and the balance is distributed in accordance with the will. If there is no will, provincial family law will apply.

How Much Insurance to Sell?

(a) Capitalization of Income Method: Annual Income/Real Rate of Interest = 50,000/85-2% (e.g.) = $833,333.

(b) Capital Retention Method: considers assets and liabilities *while realizing that some assets will not be sold upon the death of the first spouse:*

(i) Assets:	Death Benefit	$2,500
	Investments	$200,000
	Cash	$80,000

Home

Cottage

       TOTAL   <u>$282,500</u>.

(ii) Final Expenses: Funeral $20,000

       Legal and Accounting $ 10,000

       Taxes $150,000

       Home

       Cottage

       Mortgage $500,000

       Debts   <u>$30,000</u>

Total Final Expenses   <u>$710,000</u>

Cash Need = 710K – 282.5K = 427.5K

(iii) Income Needs

	Husband Dies	Wife Dies
Total Annual Income	53,400	108,400

144

Total Annual Expenses   61,000   61,000

Difference   - 7,600   47,400

Assumption: Interest Rate   6%   6%

F/Interest Rate   -126,667(G)

Insurance Need   -554,167   -427,500

The insurance contract must be in writing and must include the application, plus all documents written so far; the death benefit may be payable via a lump sum or installments/interest only until a specified age or a life annuity may be specified, depending on what the owner chooses. If the owner does not specify this, the beneficiary can do so.

The agent must witness the owner's and the life insured's signature on the application, which also asks for permission to access the MIB database (set up by insurance companies and including medical and other info, e.g., driving offenses in North America of anyone who has applied for insurance coverage). If you answer "No" to all questions on the temporary insurance agreement, i.e., diseases, medical procedures, and driving violations, and if you are younger than 65, the agent will collect the first premium and provide coverage of up to 500K for 90 days or less, but subject to cash or check encashment. If the owner dies within 90 days, the underwriter will check the answers, and if they are acceptable, the death benefit will be paid.

The insurance company must ensure an insurable interest, the need for insurance, the financial ability to pay premiums, health, and necessary medical tests (by the company's doctor, i.e., an attending physician statement, if necessary), MIB info, motor vehicle report, etc. and possible inspections regarding lifestyle, drugs, and other matters, by an investigative agency appointed by the insurance company on any project.

Claims Process

The beneficiary must present the life insured's death certificate, proof of age (usually birth certificate), and the beneficiary's claim form. The claim will generally be settled within 90 days.

Disability Insurance

Disability insurance coverage is available to full-time employees (Morbidity$\neq$ Mortality tables). It provides for a replacement of income for disability through injury (mandatory) or mental/physical sickness (optional) but may be subject to a medical examination if applying for the sickness element. The insurance benefit covers salary, commissions, net research grants, and net business income, usually between 60 and 70 % of income but not exceeding $5,000. This type of insurance coverage is important for self-employed individuals because they do not have any workers' compensation or unemployment insurance, and their Canada pension plan disability coverage is limited.

Disability is defined as the inability to perform substantial functions of one's job. The insured must need supervision by a physician. *The definition of disability varies between firms, and the insurance company can cancel the policy unless the policy is guaranteed non-cancellable. Moreover, if the policy is guaranteed renewable, the terms can be changed by the insurance company only if they change the terms for the class/category of people.* If premiums are paid with after-tax dollars, the disability benefits are tax-free. Suppose the insured is less than 65 years of age. In that case, disability coverage is more important than life coverage, because of the probability of becoming disabled, as compared with the probability of dying before the age of 65.

Disability insurance on the basis of one's "own occupation," is suited to professionals. If you cannot perform the important duties of work at your own occupation, e.g., a surgeon is not allowed to operate if he or she has a wound, you will receive the disability benefit.

Disability insurance on the basis of one's "regular occupation" is suited to middle management and skilled/office workers. If you cannot perform the important duties of your occupation and do not work elsewhere, the coverage *may* pay the shortfall in income. Disability insurance on the basis of "any occupation" is suited to non-skilled workers.

If the loss of income is greater than or equal to 80%, i.e., residual disability, the policy can cover the full disability benefit. (These variables are illustrated in the table on the following page.)

Variables in a Disability Policy

Presumptive disability: Permanent loss of 2 limbs, sight, speech, hearing, paralysis, or paraplegia (paralyzed on one side). This coverage (*not offered in group disability policies*) provides the full benefit even if you work and get paid.

	Own Occupation *Highest Premium*	**Regular Occupation** *Lower Premium*	**Any Occupation** *Lowest Premium*
One Hand Crushed	√	√	√
Treatment re: Twisted Hand	√	√	x (because he can do some other job)
Work as a Consultant:	√	x	x
Return to Original Occupation:	x	x	x

√ = Will receive disability insurance benefit

Benefit period: For how long do you wish to be paid the disability benefit: 6 months / 1 year / 5 years, for each disability occurrence, or to age 65 or 70 (unless you have the lifetime extension benefit to cover you until recovery or death)? Most people recover within one year unless the case is extreme, so it is practical to have disability coverage for 1 year.

Elimination Period: The waiting period for each disability before benefits kick in. This can be longer when the employee has WSIB coverage. For policies with an 'accumulation of days' feature, consider previous waiting periods.

Recurrent Disability clause: If the second occurrence of disability is from the same/related cause and occurs within the period specified in the contract (say $\leq$ 6 months) of the original disability. It will be considered to be a continuation of the original disability, i.e., there will not be a new waiting period.

Partial Disability clause: When you cannot perform all your functions all the time or when you are recovering from total disability, which is expected not to exceed 6 months.

Residual Disability (partial, but for a more extended period): If you are totally disabled (own/regular/any) for the contractual qualification period and you partially recover, then residual disability benefit applies, in accordance with the contract. For example, consider the case of a machine operator who earns $4,000 per month, with disability coverage of $2,000 per month, who crushes one of his or her hands, rendering him or her totally disabled for 6 months. He then recovers and gets a new job for $3,000 per month. If he or she has a residual disability, he or she will receive a benefit of 25% x Disability Coverage ($2,000) per month = $500 per month. *If the loss is less than 20%, the benefit will be nil, but if the loss exceeds 80%, the full residual benefit will be paid.*

The premium will be based on occupation (professionals and skilled workers), but preexisting conditions will not be covered.

There will be no disability coverage for injury resulting from intentional acts or attempted suicide, drugs, war, impaired driving, pregnancy (unless complications prevent either spouse from working), AIDS or HIV, cosmetic surgery within 6 months of the policy being issued, mistakes during surgery, and certain other factors.

Various Riders/Disability Policies:

These riders provide coverage for accidental death and dismemberment (ADD), lifetime benefits extension, coverage after the age of 65, etc.

Concurrent disability applies to disability from more than one injury or sickness, e.g., a driving accident causes sickness and injury, in which case only one month's disability benefit will be paid. Preexisting conditions *may* be covered with a limited payment or an extended waiting period.

There are several types of disability policies and riders.

Guaranteed non-cancellable rider: the insurer cannot change anything;

Guaranteed Renewable: the insurer can change the premium for a particular class of people;

Conditionally Renewable: the insurer can renew the policy under certain conditions;

Optionally Renewable: the policy is renewable at the owner's option;

Cancellable: the insurer can cancel the policy at any time with at least 15 days' notice.

Disability income is not taxable if you pay the premiums or if the employer pays and includes the amount on your T4.

Riders: Waiver of Premium, ADB (lump sum tax-free), AD&D (lump sum tax-free), COLA for inflation but not deflation, own occupation rider for (say) 5 years, etc.

Extended Health Care

If medical coverage provided by the government (OHIP) is insufficient to cover medical care, extended health care can cover the shortfall. This is tax-free regardless of who pays the premiums, and there is a 10-day rescission period. Premiums are based on the risk attached to each class, and the terms include renewability, grace period, claims, and procedures. *Over-insurance is prohibited.*

Employment Insurance

Taxable disability benefits are payable after deducting WSIB and group disability benefits. Such benefits cover unemployment and some disabilities, but you must have worked for at least 600 hours. The elimination period is 14 days, and the benefit period is 15 weeks, with payment equal to 55% of insurable earnings, up to $42,100. The maximum benefit is $400 per week, minus deductions at source.

Canada Pension Plan (CPP)

Taxable disability benefits are payable if the disability is *severe and prolonged,* and you must have contributed to CPP in 4 of the last 6 years. The elimination period is 4 months, and the benefit is available up to the age of 65.

Dependents of up to 18 years old or up to the age of 25 years and studying full-time, and eligible disabled pensioners may receive a monthly CPP disability.

WSIB – Tax-free Disability Benefits

These disability benefits cover work-related accidents and industrial illnesses for up to 90% of eligible earnings. This includes prescriptions, medical treatment, rehabilitation, training, special clothing, and attendant care. A death benefit by way of a lump sum plus monthly benefits is payable if the employee dies within twelve months of an accident or an industrial illness. *Workmen's compensation is tax-free.*

Accident and Sickness Insurance

This benefit covers disability and medical requirements beyond OHIP prescription drugs, dental (comprehensive), vision, and emergency travel health.

Critical Illness (Living Benefit)

This benefit applies to life-threatening cancer, heart attack, stroke, coronary artery, bypass surgery, AIDS on the job, and some other medical problems. The survival period usually is at least 30 days, depending on the type of critical illness. There can be a return of premium rider to get a *tax-free* refund of premiums if there is no claim during the policy period. The policy can be a standalone policy or by way of a rider on a life insurance policy. Preexisting conditions are *not* covered.

Long-term Care Insurance (LTC)

This coverage applies if you cannot perform any two of the following functions: eating, bathing, dressing, toileting, moving, or if you suffer from cognitive impairment or mental illness. You can receive benefits of up to $10,000 per month, but only those aged 4080 years can be insured for LTC. The buyer of the policy must be between the ages of 16 and 80; e.g., a grandson can buy a policy for his grandparent who needs constant care. The benefit is paid to a professional/institution for charges incurred.

Group Insurance

– One-year term on all types of group policies.

We have looked at individual policies. Now let us review group policies, where a group is defined to include a company, partnership, association, club, sole proprietor with employees, and some other organizations. The emphasis is on the employee's income, job, hours of work, whether the employee smokes or not, and some other factors, but not on age or medical factors. The owner controls the policy and can customize it.

If the group consists of at least 25 members, there is no medical requirement.

Contribution plan: the employee contributes to premiums and may have a waiver of premium benefits with a 90-day elimination period.

Non-contribution plan: where the employer pays 100% of the premium.

There are two systems: non-refund/retention accounting and refund accounting, where excess premiums are refunded to the company. Larger companies usually prefer the latter system.

Instead of buying a group insurance policy, the company may settle claims directly, i.e., take self-insurance and retain the services of an insurance company to administer the policy for a fee.

Premium Rates

Large companies use experience rates, whereas small companies use manual or book rates, and blended rates (manual with an adjustment) are used by medium-sized groups.

Basic coverage is available without a medical examination, but additional coverage normally requires a medical examination.

This type of policy can be converted into an individual policy within 31 days of leaving the group and without a medical examination, with the rate of premium being based on age, health, and some other factors. The benefit is tax-free. For an individual policy, in the case of a misstatement of age, the death benefit will be according to actual age, less additional premiums that should have been paid if age was understated. For group life insurance, only the premium will be adjusted. The benefit may include an additional amount to help the surviving spouse for a short term after the first spouse's death.

Group Disability Insurance

If a group policy pays a benefit, the employment insurance (EI) and CPP disability benefits will be reduced. If the group policy is better than the EI policy, the company will receive a discount on EI premiums. If the employer pays the premium and does not declare it on the employee's T4 slip, the employee is taxable for the disability benefit.

Short-term disability is that of up to 17 weeks, in which case the waiting period is up to 7 days. WSIB will provide coverage for disability sustained on the job, and group insurance policy will cover disability off the job, with *own occupation* coverage up to 24 months and *any occupation* coverage up to 65 years of age of the insured.

Group Medical Insurance

This coverage is available for items not covered by OHIP, e.g., a semiprivate hospital room. If the employer contributes, he will get a tax deduction, and benefits will be tax-free to the employee.

Group Life: the death benefit is always tax-free;

Group long-term care and disability: If the employer contributes, the benefit will be taxable on the employee, so the employee may wish to contribute through a payroll deduction. The waiting or probation period varies between companies.

It usually takes 31 days from the end of the probation period to join (i.e., submit forms and report for work) a group plan. Otherwise, the employee may be subject to a medical examination and other requirements

Group accident and sickness plans: see information on this subject provided previously.

Coordination of Benefits: The companies that offer benefits will liaise on group plans, EI, CPP, and WSIB; one cannot receive a disability benefit in excess of one's gross income lost from all sources. If a policy has a CPP offset, the government will pay the CPP benefit first, and the group policy will pay the balance. If the insurance company compensates you and you also receive disability benefits from another source, you *must* return the latter to the insurance company, *or the insurance company may sue the negligent party and give you a lump sum after deducting amounts paid to you!* This is referred to as *a subrogation of rights.*

For example, a single deductible of $50, a family deductible of $150, and coinsurance of 80%

Self: Claim for $1,000 – settlement for ($1,000 – 50) *80%

Next: Family Claim for $1,000 (1000-100) *80%

Tom	**Tanya**
50/150/80%	100/200/80%
No Co-ordination of Benefits	Co-ordination of Benefits

The first claim must legally go to Tom because there is no coordination of benefits.

The company that has opted out of CHLIA becomes the first payer. If both plans have coordination of benefits, then the claim must first be presented to the company that employs the disabled person and then the claim may be submitted to the spouse's company, if necessary. If children are making a claim, then look at the parent whose birthday falls earlier in the year; if both spouses have the same date, then proceed alphabetically on the basis of first names. If the parents are divorced, then the claim will go to the custodial parent before going to the other parent.

In the case of joint custody, the claim first goes to the parent with whom the child is living at the time of disability. The claim goes to the custodial parent, then to her spouse, then to the biological father, and then to his spouse.

25 Family Disability 80%	**25 Disability 100%**
Bob	Joan
No Co-ordination	Co-ordination
151*80% = 120.80	30.20

Insurance Industry Regulations

Some regulations govern deposits to be placed by insurance companies, based on the face value of insurance policies issued, reinstatement of insurance policies, contract information, and unfair practices (e.g., churning: replacing with an inferior policy from the same company; twisting:

replacing with an inferior policy from a different company), licensing and continuing education.

Rebating

Referral fees should be a fixed dollar amount rather than a percentage, but you can split a percentage with another licensed agent. A replacement of an insurance policy needs a disclosure statement in four copies: one for the old insurance company, one for the new insurance company, one for the client, and one for the agent. The old policy must **not** be cancelled until the new policy comes into force.

Errors and omissions coverage is mandatory for agents but does not cover fraud or criminal intent.

Holding out: an agent's image must be professional. The insurance company's legal department must approve advertisements and one cannot present oneself as being a leading agent of the company.

There is usually an organization that offers policyholders some degree of assurance for their insurance coverage in the event that the insurer fails to meet its obligations.

Rating Agencies include S&P, AM BEST, and Moody's. These organizations rate firms on the basis of profits, reserves, claims, debts, and operations.

Investments/Financial Instruments

Cash: Cash and short-term borrowings, such as treasury bills issued by the government to financial institutions and corporations, provincial and municipal papers, banker's acceptances, commercial paper, and bonds (issued by the govt. or corporations. at face value/premium/discount with a specified interest rate, payment schedule, and maturity date).

Stocks/Shares: Equity and Preferred shares are normally issued by corporations in an attempt to raise funds for the business enterprise.

Mutual Funds (MF) may be fixed-income mutual funds: treasury bills, bonds, debentures, or growth mutual funds: equity, debentures, or balanced (i.e., a combination of both). Mutual funds represent a pool of money: a diversified investment managed by a professional portfolio manager, i.e., active management (as opposed to indexed = impassive management, with lower management fees). The company from which you buy the mutual fund can sell the funds on your instructions, but this is regulated by the Securities Act and the Securities Commission. A mutual fund license is needed to sell; the sale is prospectus-based, and the Securities Commission must approve the prospectus. The owners are unit holders and are protected by CIPF from losses due to the bankruptcy of MF sellers, who are members of the IDA. Comingling is not permitted: MF companies must invest monies in a trust account rather than misuse the funds in question.

Net Asset Value and ACB are always important.

Volatility, risk, and rate of return determine the investments: money market funds have low risk/return, bond funds have medium risk/return, equity funds are more aggressive, mortgage funds invest in residential mortgages with CMHC insurance to cover o/s mortgages, where necessary, real estate funds invest in residential and commercial properties, specialty funds invest in particular sectors: technology, healthcare, transportation, etc.

Asset allocation is determined by whether you want a fixed income, growth, or balanced returns.

Segregated Funds, Individual Variable Insurance Contracts (IVIC), Individual Variable Deferred Annuity, or Individual Annuity Contracts are regulated by the Insurance Act. Insurance contracts are creditor-proof, tax-free to the beneficiary, and probate does not apply to them.

Segregated funds are mutual funds with insurance features: owner, insured, annuitant. The benefit does not go to probate on death, but there is no rescission period. One needs a life license to sell to holders of a SIN# (or someone who has had a SIN# at one point in time), who must be less than 80 years of age.

Advertisements regarding segregated funds must follow the guidelines of the Canadian Life and Health Insurance Association (CLHIA). If the fund is at least 10 years old, you must show the 1,3, 5, and 10-year performance information. The owner of the fund contract is the insurance company that issues the segregated funds. The segregated fund contract stipulates a 10-year holding period, after which the contract matures. If there is one deposit to the segregated fund, then the maturity is 10 years from that date.

If there is a series of deposits, you must follow the terms of the contract, e.g., deposits as follows: 1st Jan 2005: $10,000; 1st March 2005: $5000 … 1st October 2006: $6000 … then maturity is on 31st December 2016.

The guarantee is at least 75% of the deposit, but only if you cash out on the maturity date or death, otherwise, there is no guarantee, but only a valuation. Therefore, a segregated fund is an insurance holding.

Younger people will go for a 75%/75% guarantee re: maturity/death, middle-aged people will go for a 75%/100% guarantee, and older people will go for a 100%/100% guarantee. When a segregated fund matures in 10 years, you can change from 75/75 to 75/100 or 100/100 depending on suitability to age and other factors.

If the segregated fund is an RSP, the owner is the annuitant. Segregated funds that are not mutual funds are protected from creditors, *if the beneficiary is in the preferred class*.

The guarantee of at least 75% can be reset to market value, but maturity will be 10 years from that date. If you withdraw before 10 years, then the $\geq$ 75% guarantee will apply only to the segregated fund balance; penalties apply unless the segregated fund contract allows such withdrawals.

There are two methods of calculating the revised $\geq$ 75% guarantee. The linear method is suited to funds with an interest base, whereas the proportional method is suited to funds with an equity base. If one follows the linear method, the withdrawal is deducted from the cost/reset value, but if one follows the proportional method, one looks at the withdrawal/market value x 100. This means that if the market value goes down, you should use the linear method, but if the market value goes up, you should adopt the proportional method because you will receive more money.

Where the insurance company reinvests the distributions/allocations, you will receive a tax slip, and the tax paid increases will increase your ACB. Allocations are time-weighted, unlike those that relate to mutual funds. Capital losses are allocated to the investor, unlike in the case of mutual funds. Loads could be frontloads, backloads, DSc or a combination. However, there can be no DSc after 7 years. Negotiation is possible only for front-end loads, and you must know the calculation. There is no rescission, and valuation is at net asset value.

Market value adjustment: the longer the period of the investment, the higher the return; e.g., the GIC percentage rate is higher for longer periods of investment.

Probate

On death, one's estate is frozen and managed by the appointed executor, e.g., a family member or trust company, who must pay the income taxes + half of the capital gains (considered to be income, unless rolled over by naming the spouse as beneficiary) + probate tax/fees. The executor must obtain a clearance certificate from the Canada Revenue Agency, then pay creditors and follow the terms of the will of the deceased person. If there is no will, the executor must follow provincial family law.

Annuity

An annuity is an insurance product that is creditor-proof and to which probate does not apply. This consists of a series of payments to the annuitant at regular intervals and is conceptually the reverse of a mortgage. In the case of a term or term-certain annuity, banks, financial institutions, and insurance companies can sell, but single or multi-life annuities can only be sold by insurance companies, e.g., RSP, RRIF, etc.

An *immediate*, as opposed to a deferred annuity, is one which makes its first payment within 12 months. The period before payment is the accumulation period, and growth is taxed unless it is part of an RSP; a segregated fund is always treated as a deferred annuity. There is no suicide clause because it is the investor's money that has been deposited, and there is a beneficiary, unlike in the case of GICs.

The valuation date is the maturity date, with no rescission period.

Term annuity versus life annuity. In the case of a life annuity, if you die during the annuity term, the beneficiary will receive a lump sum or annuity.

Straight Life Annuity

This type of annuity is for people who expect to live a long time. If you die, there is no death benefit: (a) Joint Life Annuities, e.g., Joint and Last Survivor, and (b)

Guaranteed Minimum Term Life Annuities: if a guarantee is 5 years and you die in (for example) 3 years, the beneficiary will receive a 2year annuity. The annuity may or may not be in an RSP or other registered savings plan.

A *non-registered* annuity can be a prescribed annuity: level payment including capital and interest if Canada Revenue Agency conditions are met or an "accrued" annuity: a major portion of the payment will be interest in the early years, and therefore taxable income. Registered annuities are fully taxable upon withdrawal.

An annuity can be indexed according to the Cost of Living (COLA), meaning that every year, you will receive a different payment depending on the change in the cost of living index.

An annuity can be a variable annuity, an impaired annuity (for people with health problems), or a structured settlement, e.g., if you have an accident, the insurance company pays you a monthly annuity.

Factors that affect annuity payments include the interest rate, term and frequency of payment, age, gender, single or joint account status, and the guarantee factor.

Retirement

The government has certain programs in place:

(a) Canada Pension Plan (CPP) (if you apply) is a taxable benefit based on contributions (the first $3,500 is CPP-free) for at least 10 years. If you die, the benefit goes to your spouse and dependent children younger than 18 (or 25 if in full-time education). If you retire before the age of 65, the benefit will be reduced by ½% per month of age less than 65 years and increased analogously for retirement after the age of 65.

(b) Old Age Security (OAS) (if you apply) is a taxable benefit if you are at least 65 years old and a resident of 10 years, but clawbacks apply for income over $62,144, and this benefit is not transferable to your spouse or children if you die.

(c) Guaranteed Income Supplement is tax-free if you are receiving OAS and have a low income. *The allowance is tax-free to spouses between the ages of 60 and 64 if you are receiving OAS and GIS.*

For RSPs, the accumulation room or limit is 18% of the previous year's earned income plus the unused brought forward room minus the pension adjustment (PA)/contribution minus the past service PA; for an RSP account, the bank must know who the contributor, annuitant, and beneficiary are.

Own His Spousal RSP

Contributor Self-Self

Annuitant/Owner Self-Spouse

Beneficiary AA

Contribution to a spousal RSP depends on how much room a person has. One ignores the spouse's income if the lower-income spouse withdraws from the spousal RSP in the year of contribution or up to 2 years thereafter. The withdrawal is initially taxed on the higher-income spouse, but after 2 years, the withdrawal is taxed on the lower-income spouse.

If you have a younger income spouse, you can keep contributing to her RSP even after you reach the age of 71. Canada Revenue Agency applies the LIFO method.

(a) Qualified investments do not include gems, precious stones, uncertified gold and silver bars, real estate, shares in a corporation where you have at least a 10% holding;

(b) Earned income includes salary, bonuses, commissions, royalty income, net rental income, alimony less professional and union dues;

(c) You can c/fwd. RSP contributions to a future year if you expect to be in a higher tax bracket;

(d) Maximum over contribution without penalty is $2,000 as an excess balance. Still, you do not get a tax deduction for the excess payment. There is a penalty of 1% per month for excess contributions *unless you obtain the necessary* Canada Revenue Agency *form stamped by the* Canada Revenue Agency *and present it to the trustee of your RSP.* If you withdraw from your RSP, you cannot get back the initial "RSP room" unless you take advantage of:

(i) the Home Buyer's Plan (HBP), whereby you can withdraw up to $20,000 as a down payment if you and your spouse have not owned a home for the past 5 years. You can repay the HBP in 15 equal annual installments from Year 2 onwards: designate these as HBP payments on each occasion; otherwise, they will be treated as taxable income or

(ii) a Lifelong Learning Plan of up to $20,000 in total over 4 years (with a $10,000 cap in any year) if you are attending a full-time course.

RSPs mature on 31 December of the year in which you turn 71, at which time you should convert to an annuity or RRIF and pay tax on amounts received. Otherwise, the RSP will be considered to be withdrawn and will be taxed as income on withdrawal/death unless one's spouse is named as the beneficiary, in which case the amount will be taxed on her withdrawal or death.

Registered Retirement Income Fund (RRIF)

Annual withdrawals in line with the minimum amounts laid down by Canada Revenue Agency tables are as follows: fair market value (FMV) of a RRIF on January 1 following retirement is $400K, and withdrawal is based on your/your spouse's age, but you must specify which one, for the life of the RRIF. The first minimum annual withdrawal = 1/ 90 years – 70 years = 5% of FMV; the second minimum annual withdrawal = 1/90 – 71 = 5.33% of FMV; the third annual minimum withdrawal = 1/90 – 72 = 5.67% of FMV, etc. After the age of 89, there will be 5 equal annual installments.

An RRIF can be closed at any time.

On death, the fair market value of the RRIF is considered to be taxable income unless it is transferred to the *beneficiary* spouse's **RSP/RRIF/annuity** or beneficiary child/grandchild <18 years old who will receive taxable equal installments up to age 18 or beneficiary handicapped child/stepchild/grandchild by way of an annuity or RSP for him or her.

Registered Plans

You can contribute from any age if you have earned income, e.g., modeling or acting role income or royalty income up to the end of the year in which you turn 71; if withdrawn at 65 or 60 years old, there will be a deduction of 6% p.a. (as for CPP).

The contribution room considers RSP plus the pension deduction of the employee and employer:

1. Defined Benefit Plans. Employers and employees contribute to a professionally managed fund to give you a specific amount upon retirement. For example, it could be a 1.5% Defined Benefit Plan considering years of service; e.g., John has worked for 30 years and has a 1.5% DBP.

Career average plan: 1.5% of average income $50,000. Therefore, the defined benefit is 1.5% x $50,000 x 30 years = $22,500 per year.

Best 5 years-plan

Last 5 years-plan

Fixed benefit plan: fixed percentage contribution for employees and variable contribution from the employer, both of which are deductible.

2. Defined Contribution Plans. Fixed contributions by employer and employee. After the specified period, contributions become vested and can grow or be transferred

to another plan or LIRA (locked-in retirement account until the rules of the plan allow withdrawals)/LIF/LRIF with spousal consent. The LIF must be converted to a life annuity before 31 December of the year in which you turn 80.

If an employee leaves before the plan becomes vested, i.e., within 2 years, then the amount in his or her plan will be transferred to company profits via a deferred (profit) sharing plan; if vested, he or she can leave the money with the same company or take it to his or her new employer or convert it to a LIRA, LIF or LRIF.

Government Benefits

The Canada Pension Plan provides pension, disability, survivor pension for spouse, allowance for orphaned children, and death benefit ($2,500 or 6 months' pension). Contributions are mandatory if your annual earnings are $3,500$42,100.

Contributions: 4.95% by the employee and 4.95% by the employer; maximum CPP is $850 per month from age 65 onwards; if you retire early, CPP is 6% less p.a. Therefore, if you retire at 60, you get $850 per month.

Less 30% = approx. $600 per month. If you retire at 70, you get 6% more p.a.

CPP is taxable; income splitting is allowed, as for RSP contributions

Old Age Security (OAS) is a taxable federal benefit but you must be 65 years old and have been a resident for at least 10 years after the age of 18 years, with citizenship or landed immigrant status. The full OAS is approximately $500 per month if you have lived in Canada for at least 40 years.

If net annual taxable income is more than $63,511, OAS will be reduced by 15% for the amount exceeding $63,511, in accordance with the table specified by the Canadian government.

OAS with pensions of less than $14,256 will be given a guaranteed income supplement of approximately $7,200, with a higher allowance to a surviving spouse from the death of the other spouse if he or she is between 6064 years of age.

RESPs

Parents or grandparents can start contributing $2,000 p.a. (or up to $4,000 to catch up on a 1-year backlog) from the child's birth until 21 years of age. A CESG grant of 20% supplements this, but the total contribution must be at least $42,000, and the maximum CESG is $7,200. The child can begin withdrawing from this as taxable income from the age of 18 years for university or college education; the plan collapses 25 years after the initial contribution, and if the child does not pursue education, the CESG grant will be clawed back, and RESP of up to $50K can be transferred to your RSP or spousal RSP; the balance will be taxed as income, with a 20% penalty if the RESP is equal to or more than 10 years old.

Home Buyer's Plan (HBP)

If you are a new home buyer or have not owned a house for 5 years and you have money in an RSP for at least 90 days, you can withdraw up to $20,000 but must repay the loan within 17 years of the end of the year in which you took the HBP. For example, if you took the HBP in 2007, begin paying 1/15 back from 2010 onwards. Otherwise, the 1/15 will be taxed as income, from 2010 onwards.

Taxation

Canada has a progressive system of taxation: the higher the income, the higher the tax payable, with brackets being adjusted for inflation; dividends are preferable to interest, and capital gains are preferred to dividends and interest. Tax credits, such as for charitable donations, are normally better than tax deductions. Also

(a) Fair market value is important for deemed dispositions: death, related party transactions, switches, and gifts;

(b) If the man/woman has a cottage, assume it is a second property unless mentioned otherwise;

(c) Term 100 Joint Last to Die is best for estate planning to pay off taxes and transfer property tax-free to family; only RSP without beneficiary rolls over to spouse, and permanent residence transfers tax-free to any family member. A 500K small business capital gain exemption p.a. applies on sale of one's own private corporation or farm shares in a public corporation

(d) Charitable giving: donation to a Canada Revenue Agency-approved charity gives you a tax credit on premiums, cash value and even death benefit of policy donated to charity. There are no probate fees on death benefit that goes into the estate for transfer to charity, but one needs a receipt for donations to the Canada Revenue Agency-approved charity.

Estate Equalization

This is an attempt to ensure fair treatment of beneficiaries when liquidity is low because of executor's fees, probate fees, and other factors. There should be adequate insurance coverage, e.g., Term 100, to ensure liquidity in the estate.

Risk Management

You may reduce or avoid the risk, share/transfer the risk with (say) an insurance company, invest in a balanced fund, or take the risk.

Agency Law

An agent can bind a principal in various circumstances: an insurance agent has 2 principals, employer, and client, whose needs he must address through

(a) disclosure and recommendations honestly and without duress, otherwise ≠ contract;

(b) ongoing administrative duties: delivering policy, making changes re: address, bank info, birth in the family, monitoring needs by keeping in touch; and

(c) conscientious attitude and maintaining client confidentiality.

Theft: it is advisable to accept checks rather than cash – do not use client's monies

Replace policies only if beneficial to the client.

Errors and Omissions coverage protects against torts that are not crimes, e.g., fraud or forgery.

Business Continuation Insurance

This type of coverage helps a client to continue business in the event of the death or disability of a shareholder/partner, etc. There must be a buy-sell agreement that states the basis of the valuation and buyout of the disabled/deceased partner. The buyout can be financed by an insurance policy.

(i) Cross-purchase agreement: a prospective buyer can buy a policy on a prospective seller of a business or

(ii) Crisscross purchase agreement: partners can buy policies on one another or

(iii) Share redemption agreement: the business buys policies on shareholders/partners and pays the disability/death benefit to the beneficiary/estate.

Disability buyouts have a long waiting period of, for example, 2 years to ensure that the disability in question is permanent. Many companies buy life insurance and/or disability insurance for key employees.

Business Overhead Expense Insurance

This type of coverage helps to pay rent, salaries other than the owner's, utilities for, e.g., 2 years of disability, and some other expenses in order to help pay for business operations while the owner/manager is disabled.

T10 = Term Insurance for 10 years

T20 = Term Insurance for 20 years

R and C = Renewable and Convertible

Non-Con = Non-convertible

Non-par = Non-participation permanent Policy

Par = participating permanent insurance policy

Joint 1st = Joint First to Die

Joint 2nd = Joint Second to Die

Bibliography

Ambrecht, John. *Estate Planning for the Family Business: The Non-Linear Approach.* Santa Barbara, CA: Ambrecht and Associates, 2001.

American Psychological Association. *Anger Class.* Washington, DC: Author, 2006. Retrieved from http://www.angerclassonline.com

Anderson, Eugene W. and Claes Fornell. A customer satisfaction research prospectus, in R. T. Rust and R. L. Oliver (eds), *Service Quality: New Directions in Theory and Practice* (241268). Thousand Oaks, CA: Sage, 1994.

Ball, Bruce, Garry Duncan and P. Leach. *Family Business.* Toronto: Thomson Carswell, 2003.

BBC News. Crowe 'deserved to be exposed'. June 20, 2002. Retrieved from http://news.bbc.co.uk/2/hi/entertainment/2055286.stm

BBC News. Crowe jokes about phone incident. November 28, 2005. Retrieved from http://news.bbc.co.uk/2/hi/entertainment/4477178.stm

BDO Dunwoody. *Your Family Business Matters*. Toronto BDO, 2002.

Belding, Shaun. Dealing with the Customer from Hell. Toronto: Stoddart, 2000.

Bellenger, Danny N., Earle Steinberg, and Wilbur Stanton. The congruence of store image and self-image: as it relates to store loyalty. *Journal of Retailing, 52* (Spring 1976), 1732.

Berry, Leonard L. Relationship marketing, in L.L Berry, G. L. Shostack and G.D. Upah (eds. *Emerging Perspectives on Services Marketing* (2528). Chicago, IL: American Marketing Association.

Blanchard, K., and Bowles, S. M. Raving Fans: *A Revolutionary Approach to Customer Service*. New York, NY: William Morrow and Company, 1993.

Blanchard, Ken. *Leadership Smarts*. New York: Honor Books, UK, 2004.

Blasingame, Jim. *The Color of Ethics Is Gray – Part Two*. April 15, 2003. Retrieved from http://www. smallbusinessadvocate.com/smallbusinessarticles/thecol orofethicsisgraypartone236

Borden, Ladner. "It Begins with Service" (PowerPoint Presentation). Toronto: Gervais, 2008.

Bowen, D.E. & R. B. Chase. "Philosophy of Marketing," in *Service Management Effectiveness* (299323), edited by T. G. Cummings. San Francisco, CA: JosseyBass, 2008.

Bowen, John. Development of a taxonomy of services to gain strategic relationship marketing, in T. L. Childers, R. P. Bagozzi et al. (eds), *1989 AMA Winter Educators' Conference: Marketing Theory and Practice* (216220). Chicago, IL: AMA, 1990.

Brown, D.R. and A.N. Angee. *The Living Franklin*. Oak Brook, IL: Oakbrook, 1975.

Carol, F. and Michael R. Solomon. Predictability and personalization in the service encounter. *Journal of Marketing, 51* (April 1987), 8696.

CNN. Russell Crowe appears in court – Actor arrested on charges related to phone throwing incident. June 6, 2005. Retrieved from_______http://www.cnn.com/2005/ SHOWBIZ/Movies /06/06/crowe.arrest/

Cronin, J. Joseph, Jr. and Steven A. Taylor, Measuring service quality: A reexamination and extension. *Journal of Marketing, 56* (July 1992), 5568.

Crosby, Lawrence A., Kenneth Evans, and Deborah Cowles. Relationship quality in services selling: An interpersonal influence perspective. *Journal of Marketing, 54* (July 1990), 6881.

Czepiel, John A. "Managing Relationships with Customers: A Differentiation Philosophy of Marketing," edited by D.E. Bowens, R.B. Chase and T.G. Cummings. 1990.

Czepiel, John A. and Robert Gilmore (1987), "Exploring the Concept of Loyalty in Services," in J.A. Czepiel, C.A. Congram and J. Shanahan (eds), *The Services Marketing Challenge: Integrating for Competitive Advantage* (9194). Chicago, IL: AMA, 1987.

Day, George S. A two-dimensional concept of brand loyalty. *Journal of Advertising Research, 9* (September 1971), 2936.

DeCotiis, Allen R. and Paul Singer. The value of the ideal customer experience, ServiceSat.com. *Phoenix Marketing International*, Fall 2001.

Dick, Alan S. and Kunal Basu. Customer loyalty: Toward an integrated conceptual framework. *Journal of the Academy of Marketing Science, 22* (Spring 1994), 99113.

Drucker, Peter F. *The Daily Drucker.* New York: HarperCollins, 2004.

Dwyer, F. Robert, Paul H. Schurr, and Sejo Oh. Developing buyer seller relationships. *Journal of Marketing, 51* (April 1987), 1127.

Edersheim, Elizabeth. *The Definitive Drucker.* New York McGraw Hill, 2007.

Fornell, Claes. A national customer satisfaction barometer: The Swedish experience. *Journal of Marketing, 56* (January 1992), 621.

Fredrickson, J.W. The comprehensiveness of strategic decision processes: Extension, observations, future directions. *Academy of Management Journal, 27*(3) (1984), 445457.

Green, Patrick. *Family Wealth and Business Succession Planning.* New York: OSCPA, 2007.

Gremler, D. & S. Brown. Service Loyalty: Its Nature, Importance, and Implications. University of Idaho.

Hamm, B.A. Want a company you can be truly proud of? Try a business ethics program. *Compass Solutions*, 2003. Retrieved Aug. 17, 2007 from http://www. compassolutions.biz/id25.htm/

Handy, Charles. *Inside Organizations.* London: Penguin, 1990.

Jacoby, Jacob and Robert W. Chestnut. *Brand Loyalty: Measurement and Management.* New York, NY: John Wiley and Sons, 1978.

Jain, Arun K., Christian Pinson, and Naresh K. Malhotra, Customer loyalty as a construct in the marketing of banking services. *International Journal of Bank Marketing, 5* (3) (1987), 4972.

Jarvis, Lance P. and James B. Wilcox. Repeat purchasing behavior and attitudinal brand loyalty: Additional evidence, in K. L. Bernhardt (ed.), *Marketing: 17761976 and Beyond* (151152). Chicago, IL: American Marketing Association, 1976.

Johnson, Michael P. Social and cognitive features of the dissolution of commitment to relationships, in S. Duck (ed.), *Personal Relationships, Volume 4: Dissolving Personal Relationships* (5173). New York, NY: Academic Press, 1982. 5173.

King, Patricia. *Never Work for a Jerk!* New York: Dorset Press, 1987.

Klemperer, Paul. Markets with consumer switching costs. *The Quarterly Journal of Economics, 102* (May 1987), 375394.

Kuratko, D.F. Strategic choices. *Journal of Small Business Management, 31*(2) (1993), 3850.

Lee, Barrett A. and Carol A. Zeiss. Behavioral commitment to the role of sport consumer: An exploratory analysis. *Sociology and Social Research, 64* (April 1980), 405419.

Leland, K. and K. Bailey. Customer Service for Dummies. Foster City, John Wiley & Sons, New York 1995.

Lincoln, Yvonna S. and Egon G. Guba. *Naturalistic Inquiry.* Newbury Park, CA: Sage Publications, 1985.

Lyles, M.A., J.S. Baird, and J.B. Orris. *Formalized Planning in Small Business: Increasing Strategic Choices*. Oxford, Blackwell Publishing, 1994.

Lynch, A. *All in the Family Inc.* Toronto: Macmillan, 2001.

Marcus Z. Cox, Stephen F., Alicia B. Gresham and Stephen F.The Role of Customer Service in Small Business Strategic Planning. Pennsylvania State University, Pennsylvania, 1997.

McCormack, Mark. *Staying Street Smart in the Internet Age*. New York, NY: Viking Penguin, 2000.

McGee, J.E. When WalMart comes to town: A look at how local merchants respond to the retailing giant's arrival. *Journal of Business and Entrepreneurship*, 8(1) (1996), 4352.

McNamara, C. Complete Guide to Ethics Management: An Ethics Toolkit for Managers. Retrieved from http://www. managementhelp.org/ethics/ethxgde.html

McParland, Kelly. $200m is more than an "error." *National Post*, 22 September 2009. Retrieved from http://www. nationalpost.com/news/story.html?id=2017800

Miller, Danny and Isabelle Miller. *Managing for the Long Run: Lessons in Competitive Advantage from Great Family Businesses. New York*: Harvard Business School Press and McGraw Hill, 2005.

Monroe, Kent B. and Joseph P. Guiltinan. A pathanalytic exploration of retail patronage influences. *Journal of Consumer Research, 2* (June 1975), 1928.

Moorhead, G. and R.W. Griffin. *Organizational Behavior*, 4th ed. Boston, MA: Houghton Mifflin, 1995.

Murray, Keith B. A test of services marketing theory: Consumer information acquisition activities. *Journal of Marketing, 55* (January 1991), 1025.

Newman, Joseph W. and Richard A. Werbel. Multivariate analysis of brand loyalty for major household appliances. *Journal of Marketing Research, 10* (November 1973), 404409.

NTA Rand Council. Family Succession Planning. NTA, 2001.

Oliva, Terence A., Richard L. Oliver and Ian C. MacMillan. A catastrophe model for developing service satisfaction strategies. *Journal of Marketing, 56* (July 1992), 8395.

Oliver, Richard L. and Gerald Linda. Effect of satisfaction and its antecedents on consumer preference and intention, in K. B. Monroe (ed.), *Advances in Consumer Research*, Vol. 8 (8893). Ann Arbor, MI: Association for Consumer Research, 1981.

Ostrowski, Peter L., Terrence O'Brien and Geoffrey Gordon. Service quality and customer loyalty in the commercial airline industry. *Journal of Travel Research, 32* (Fall 1993), 1624.

Parasuraman, A., Valarie A. Zeithaml, and Leonard L. Berry. A conceptual model of service quality and its implications for future research. *Journal of Marketing, 49* (Fall 1985), 4150.

Patsuris, Penelope., Corporate Scandal Sheet, Forbes, New York, 2002.

Pilkington, Ed. Bernard Madoff avoids jail. *The Guardian*, 12 January 2009. Retrieved from http://www.guardian.co. uk/business/2009/jan/13/madoffbaildecision

Pinto, Maxwell. *Leadership: Flirting with Disaster!* North Carolina: RoseDog Books, 2005.

Pinto, Maxwell. *Management: Tidbits for the New Millennium.* New York: Xlibris, 2008.

Pinto, Maxwell. *The Management Syndrome: How to Deal with It!* Bloomington: Xlibris, 2009.

Porter, M. E. *Competitive Strategy for Analyzing Industries and Competitors.* New York, NY: The Free Press, 1980.

Prasad, Samantha. Tax and Family Business Succession Planning.Toronto: CCH, 2007.

Pringle, Gill. Russell Crowe: "Angry? Me? Never." *The Independent,* November 7, 2008. Retrieved from http:// www.independent.co.uk/artsentertainment/films/ features/ russellcroweangrymenever997593.ht

Pritchard, Mark P. Development of the psychological commitment instrument (PCI) for measuring travel service loyalty. Doctoral dissertation, University of Oregon, 1991.

Quinn, R. Moments of greatness: Entering the fundamental state of leadership. *Harvard Business Review* (JulyAugust 2005), 7583.

Reichheld, Fred. The one number you need to grow. *Harvard Business Review*, December 2003.

Reichheld, Frederick F. Loyalty based management. *Harvard Business Review, 71* (March April 1991), 6473.

Reynolds, Fred D., William R. Darden, and Warren S. Martin. Developing an image of the store loyal customer: A lifestyle analysis to probe a neglected market. *Journal of Retailing, 50* (Winter 1975), 7384.

Satmetrix Systems, Inc. *Customer Experience Management Best Practices – Profitable Growth through Customer Centricity*. 2005. Retrieved from http://www.satmetrix. com/satmetrix/pdfs/smwpCEMbestpractices.pdf

Savage, Jack. *The Everything Home Based Business Book*. Avon, MA: Adams Media Corporation, 2000.

Saxby, David. *Measure X*. Retrieved from www.measurex.com.

Scarratt, Malcolm. *Business Succession Planning for Financial Advisors*. Toronto: CCH, 2002.

Schwass, Joachim. *Wise Growth Strategies in Leading Family Businesses.* Basingstoke, Hampshire, United Kingdom: Palgrave Macmillan, 2005.

Sheth, Jagdish N. A factor analytic model of brand loyalty. *Journal of Marketing Research, 5* (November 1968), 395404.

Silverman, Stephen M. Judge tosses out Crowe plotters' case. *People Magazine*, June 24, 2002. Retrieved from http://www.people.com/people/article/0,,624140,00.html

Silverman, Stephen M. Russell Crowe calls phone toss overplayed. *People Magazine*, November 3, 2006. Retrieved from http://www.people.com/people/article/0,,1554602,00.html

Silverman, Stephen M. Russell Crowe mocks phone throwing incident. *People Magazine*, November 28, 2005. Retrieved from http://www.people.com/people/article /0,1134863,00.html

Silverman, Stephen M. Russell Crowe sorry for 'shameful' conduct. *People Magazine*, June 9, 2005. Retrieved from http://www.people.com/people/article/0,,1070328,00

Snyder, Don R. Service loyalty and its measurement: A preliminary investigation, in M. Venkatesan, D. M. Schmalensee, and C. Marshall, eds. *Creativity in Service Marketing: What's New, What Works, What's Developing* (4448). Chicago, IL: AMA, 1986.

The Superficial. Russell Crowe finally settles phone incident. Author, November 18, 2005. Retrieved fromhttp://www.thesuperficial.com/archives/2005/11/18/russel_crowe_gets_sentenced.html

Trevino, L. and Nelson, K. *Corporate social responsibility and managerial ethics*. Hoboken, NJ: John Wiley and Sons, 2005.

Tucker, W.T. The development of brand loyalty. *Journal of Marketing Research*, 1 (August 1964), 3235.

Ultimate Business Library. *The Best Business Books Ever*. Bloomsbury, Cambridge, MA: Perseus, 2003.

Wallington, Patricia. How did we ever get from George Washington's "I cannot tell a lie" to "I refuse to testify"? The Fifth Amendment. Total Leadership – Ethical Behavior Is Essential. Retrieved from http://www.cio.com/article/31779/Total_Leadership_Ethical_Behaviour_Is_Essential?page=3

Walsh, Grant. *Family Business Succession.* Ottawa: KPMG Enterprise, 2008.

Ward, J. *Perpetuating the Family Business.* Basingstoke, Hampshire, United Kingdom: Palgrave Macmillan, 2004.

Wees, Aida Van. *Enhancing the Value of the Family Owned Business.* City: The Legal Outsourcing Network, 2008.

Weigl, Corina and Luanna McGowan. *Succession Planning Toolkit for Business Owners.* Toronto: The Canadian Institute of Chartered Accountants, 2006.

Wilton, David. Implementing Estate Freezes. Toronto: CCH, 2000.

Wright, P., M.J. Kroll and J. Parnell. *Strategic Management: Concepts and Cases*, 3rd Ed. Englewood Cliffs, NJ: Prentice Hall, 1996.

Zeithaml, Valarie A. How consumer evaluation processes differ between goods and services, in J. H. Donnelly and W. R. George (eds), *Marketing of Services* (186190). Chicago, IL: American Marketing Association, 1981.

Zeithaml, Valarie A., Leonard L. Berry and A. Parasuraman. The behavioral consequences of service quality. *Journal of Marketing*, 60.